"Franny—no happened to go?"

She couldn't think of anything to say.

He moved closer and she retreated. "You've been in my head all these years," he said. "A little urchin with brown eyes and a stubborn chin." He shook his head again. "You weren't supposed to change."

Another spurt of breeze blew by, flattening her dress against her body. "You've been gone a long time, Brett." She swallowed, trying to ease the croak in her voice.

"That long?"

She swallowed again. "Long enough for me to grow up."

Fairy lights were strung in the trees, and they backlit Brett, dazzling her. "You grew up beautiful," he said.

Dear Reader

I'm a little sister. And, like many of us, I spun my share of romantic daydreams about my brother's friends. One day, I imagined, they'd see beyond the braces and the knobbly knees to the beautiful woman within.

I hate to say it never happened. As a matter of fact, even though I'm married and I've given my brother two nephews, I'm not sure *he* even realizes I've grown up. But for Francesca Milano, the heroine of THE BRIDESMAID'S BET, it's another story. Everyone is seeing her differently: her father, her four older brothers and particularly her brothers' friend, attorney Brett Swenson.

Of course, as every younger sister knows, there's that teeny tiny problem with over-protectiveness. Francesca has four brothers who've practised it all their lives, and now Brett thinks he needs to protect her from falling in love. Too bad for him; it's too late...or is it really such a bad thing after all when Brett's the one Francesca loves?

All the best,

Christie Ridgway

Christie Ridgway

THE BRIDESMAID'S BET

BY
CHRISTIE RIDGWAY

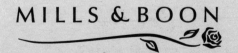

In loving memory of Judy Veisel.

First published in Great Britain 1999
Harlequin Mills & Boon Limited,
Eton House, 18-24 Paradise Road, Richmond, Surrey TW9 1SR

© Christie Ridgway 1999

ISBN 0 263 81913 2

Set in Times Roman 10½ on 13 pt.
02-0001-40020 C1

Printed and bound in Spain
by Litografia Rosés, S.A., Barcelona

1

FRANCESCA MILANO tugged her black baseball cap more firmly over her hair and stared narrowly across the kitchen at her older brother Carlo. "I spent yesterday in a bridesmaid's dress—looking like a cross between Scarlett O'Hara and something out of *Saturday Night Fever,* mind you—and now you're saying I owe you money?"

Carlo's cool expression didn't change. The fingers at the end of his outstretched palm even wiggled impatiently. "Fifty bucks."

Still reeling from her hours in puce-colored polyester over a ruffled petticoat, Francesca opened the back door to her father's apartment to let in a little air. The breeze cleared the smell of the meat-maniac pizza that was filling the stomachs of Pop and her other brothers as they watched baseball on the living room TV.

Carlo raised his eyebrows. "Stop stalling, Franny."

She did, anyway, inspecting the short fingernails she'd recently given up biting. "Who would guess that Nicky would catch the garter?" The oldest of her four brothers seemed the most firmly entrenched bachelor.

"I did," Carlo said. "The matrimony bug has bitten him bad."

Francesca frowned. Nicky *had* nearly tackled the teenager in front of him to secure the thing. But she couldn't see him *married*. "Bet he thought it would get him a shot at the maid of honor."

Carlo shook his head. "You're close to welshing on one bet already, little sister. Pay up."

She pursed her lips. At twenty-eight, Carlo was closest to her age of twenty-four and usually the kindest. "Carlo, please," she pleaded, attempting to play on his big brother heart strings—she hadn't grown up as the only female in a household of men for nothing. "I'm supposed to be going shopping with Elise later."

He went still. Then he grimaced and stretched his hand out farther. "The fifty. I'll probably need it for Nicky's wedding present."

Francesca waved the thought away. "Nicky! If we're talking weddings, I think it's my turn."

Carlo's eyes widened and his hand dropped. "Your turn for *what?*"

Francesca hadn't planned on voicing the thought, but at least Carlo was distracted from the fifty dollars she wished she didn't owe him. "Last month I was a bridesmaid, yesterday Corinne Costello dressed me up in ruffles and got married, and my best friend Elise is saying 'I do' next month. I've *got* to be up next."

"You've *got* to be kidding."

Annoyed, Francesca thrust her hands in the pockets of her jeans. "Why not me?"

Carlo rolled his eyes. "Beyond the absurdity of you

actually wishing yourself into romance-hell, there's the small fact that you haven't dated in—what?—years?''

Maybe that small fact merely underscored that it must be her turn. ''I'm going to change all that,'' she said stubbornly.

Crossing his arms over his chest, Carlo shook his head.

''I am!'' Francesca insisted.

''Tell you what, then,'' he said, a calculating smile crossing his face. ''I have another bet for you.''

Despite Carlo's crafty smile, a little thrill rushed through Francesca. Another thing growing up with brothers did was give a woman a honed sense of competition. ''Double or nothing?''

''Yeah. A hundred bucks says you can't do it.''

''Do what?'' she asked warily. No telling what Carlo, who had been unpleasantly moody the past couple of months, had up his sleeve. But she liked the idea of a chance to recoup her cash.

''I'll bet you can't get yourself a hot matrimonial prospect by—'' he paused, then snapped his fingers ''—by your next stint as bridesmaid.''

Francesca grimaced. ''What kind of bet is this, Carlo?''

His expression hardened. ''Maybe you're right. Maybe it's time…maybe we gotta get ourselves a life.''

The ''*we* gotta'' was interesting. She stared at him.

''Sheesh,'' he said. ''Forget it. Just hand over my fifty.''

"No, wait!" Thinking, Francesca clicked her nails against the tile countertop. "I don't have to pay you now?"

"Nope. But you owe me a hundred when you don't have somebody to bring to Elise's wedding at the end of the month."

That rankled. The assumption she'd lose did not sit well with a woman who had been scrambling to keep up with her four older brothers for the past twenty-four years. "Let me get this straight. A steady man in my life by Elise's wedding cancels my debt?"

Carlo nodded. And his confident smirk filled Francesca with determination.

LITTLE FRANNY MILANO on a manhunt? On the other side of the open kitchen door, Brett Swenson stood, stunned by the idea.

Of course, she must have gone from little girl to woman in the twelve years since he'd left, but still Brett couldn't resist the decades-old habit of rescuing her from sibling skullduggery.

To prevent them from finalizing their bet, Brett rapped on the doorjamb. Carlo, whom he could see clearly in profile, immediately swung his way, a grin breaking over his face.

"Brett, you old dog! You made it!"

Brett reached out to shake the other man's hand. "And ready to move in. I just stopped by to say hi and get the keys."

"Brett? Keys?" Franny said, breaking in.

Brett turned her way, for the first time getting a glimpse. She hadn't grown much. Still slight, and her features were shaded by the deep bill of a baseball cap. He let out a satisfied sigh. With all of life's unpredictability, this one thing hadn't changed. Tomboy Franny. Still the scrappy little sister he'd never had.

"Franny," he said, bending slightly and peering under the hat, trying to get a clearer look at what growing up had done to her.

She looked away from him quickly, to cock her head at her brother. "What's going on?"

Carlo grinned. "Didn't I tell you? Brett is back in San Diego. I ran into him at the D.A.'s office. He's in Apartment 7 until he decides where he wants to live permanently."

A bouncy ponytail swung from behind her ball cap as she shook her head. "Pop didn't mention anything to me."

Carlo shrugged. "You've been occupied with wedding stuff." He rubbed his palms together. "Which reminds me, Franny—"

"Do I smell pizza?" Brett interrupted, his impulse to stop their wager resurging. He remembered another Milano bet made years ago. Francesca's brothers had laid odds on how long their tag-along sister would cry once they ditched her for a boys-only bike expedition to the park.

Unable to stomach the thought of the little girl's tears,

Brett returned for her alone. After drying her grubby, tear-streaked face, she'd ridden with the dignity of a tiny tomboy princess, carefully balanced on the handlebars of his stingray bicycle.

Now she jabbed her thumb in the direction of another door, "They're all in Pop's living room—Nicky, Joe and Tony, downing a double order of a double-meat, double-cheese."

Brett almost smiled as another unfamiliar rush of all's-right-with-the-world flooded him. The decision to return to his hometown had been the right one. Eighteen months had passed since Patricia's death, and it was time to restart his life.

The Milanos were just the family to help him do it. The four Milano brothers had been like his own growing up. And Franny…

"About what we were discussing, Carlo," she said.

…had been much too young to date! "How old are you now?" he blurted out, trying to turn the conversation again.

She slanted him a look from underneath the brim of the cap, then shifted her gaze to Carlo. "Old enough to get what I want when I want it. You're on, big brother."

"CARLO'S LOST IT," Francesca's best friend, Elise, said, stopping in the department store aisle to finger a paisley scarf. "And what's wrong with you? Why'd you agree to such a bet?"

Francesca made herself touch the scarf, too. She really

had no interest in the slinky, slippery thing, but she'd promised herself to start taking some clues from Elise. Her friend, engaged to be married in a month, had also never been short of boyfriends during their growing-up years. "I agreed because the bet will finally make me do something about it."

"About what?"

"About getting that life Carlo mentioned."

Elise swung around and squinted her eyes, her gaze sweeping over Francesca. "I've been saying you need one for years."

"I know, I know. It's just—"

"That you work for your dad. That your dad manages a bunch of apartments mainly filled with senior citizens. That you don't have much opportunity to meet men. That you don't know how to attract them. That you don't know how to dress." Elise hadn't stopped for a breath, but she drew one in now. "Do I need to go on?"

Francesca smiled in apology. "What about Aunt Elizabetta? Don't I always use her as an excuse, too?"

Elise nodded, and a delicate waft of her perfume drifted by Francesca. "How could I have forgotten? And you don't have another woman to show you the ropes. Since your mother died when you were two, your only female relative is Aunt Elizabetta, otherwise known as Sister Josephine Mary of the Good Shepherd Convent."

Francesca slapped a glass display case. "That's about the size of it."

"Well if you ask me," Elise said. "It's a bunch of

hooey. I've begged since we were fourteen to do something with you.''

Elise wore her blond hair in a short, waved bob, and even in jeans and a white blouse—like now—she looked polished and pretty. Francesca sniffed again. And Elise always wore perfume.

Francesca sighed and looked down at her own clothes. Levi's. Size Carlo-at-age-thirteen. She couldn't remember if her T-shirt was a hand-me-down, too, but it advertised auto parts. Her usual ball cap was in the car, but she'd pulled her hair into a simple ponytail.

One sneaker had a hole in the toe and the lace of the other had broken twice and was knotted in two places. "Maybe I should save myself some grief and give Carlo the hundred dollars now."

Elise picked up another scarf from the display to hold it below Francesca's chin. "Bite your tongue! You just pry open your purse, pull out a credit card and I'll do the rest." She frowned. "Do you like the color rose?"

Rose? What exact shade was "rose" and how was it different from pink? "Elise…"

"Didn't you say you wanted to get a life?"

Francesca *had* said it. She *did* want to get a life. Yesterday, standing at the altar and wearing a dress—even an ugly one—for the first time in forever had made her feel womanly and lonely all at once. "I want to primp for a candlelight dinner and have a man open a door for me and feel my heart flutter when he takes my hand," she whispered.

And speaking of heart flutters... Francesca took a breath. "Guess who's back in town?" He strode into her mind's eye just like he'd walked through the door to her father's kitchen, tall and lean with dark blond hair and those memorable, startlingly blue eyes.

Elise was inspecting the label on the square of silk. "Brett Swenson."

"You know!"

"David heard from somebody in their old gang. He's joined the district attorney's office."

Elise's fiancé, David, had run with the same crowd as her brothers and Brett. Francesca swallowed and casually inspected her nails. "Why do you think he's back?"

"For love."

"What?" Francesca's voice squeaked.

Elise raised her eyebrows. "Don't you think? To recover from it. When that car killed Patricia she wore Brett's engagement ring on her finger."

Right, Francesca reminded herself. And a grieving Brett was as far from her reach as he'd been when she was a moony twelve-year-old and he a university-bound high school senior.

With a sigh she grabbed the scarf from Elise and held it up to her face herself. She looked around for a mirror. The color rose. Did she like it? She didn't know, but she had to start somewhere.

"Why am I doing this?" she murmured, briefly giving in to doubt.

"Because you want to fall in love," Elise said firmly.

No point denying it.

With iron resolve, Francesca relegated Brett Swenson to the mental pile of unsuitable males in her life labeled "Brothers and Others."

"Fall in love?" she repeated, nodding. "With all the trimmings."

BRETT TOSSED a quasi-cold bottle of beer across his new—if temporary—living room into Carlo's cupped hands. At the baseball game's seventh-inning stretch and with the San Diego Padres well ahead, Carlo, his three brothers and their father had helped Brett unload his Jeep and the trailer he'd towed from San Francisco. Brett's Apartment 7 was next door to Carlo's own apartment, and Carlo lived next door to Franny who was next door to her father. All four were in one of the complexes owned and managed by the Milano family. Actually, according to Carlo, managed by Franny and her father.

The oldest Milano brother, Nicky, was an attorney in private practice. Tony worked construction. Joe Milano was a street cop and Carlo a police detective. At thirty, Brett fell somewhere in the midst of their stair-step ages, but it was Carlo he'd always been closest to and would have professional dealings with now that he'd joined the county district attorney's office.

"I owe you guys one," Brett said, twisting the top off his own brown bottle. The other four men had already left.

Carlo drank from his beer and grimaced. "You owe

me a cold one.'' He lifted the bottle and inspected the label. "We should have stocked the fridge first instead of last.''

"Yeah.'' Brett took a swallow. "I'll make it up to all of you by springing for dinner next weekend.'' He paused. "Franny, too.''

Brett didn't know what made him bring up her name. Well, yeah, he did. That bet still bugged him. Maybe Carlo would confess the whole thing. Explain his reasoning.

Instead, the other man grunted.

Grabbing from the kitchen counter a shoebox with "Mail'' scrawled along the side, Brett tried again. "An invitation came before I left San Francisco.'' He shook the box. "David Lee and Elise Cummings, huh? Getting married?'' Apparently that wedding was the deadline for Carlo and Franny's wager.

Carlo closed his eyes and took another long swallow of beer. "Right.'' His voice was low and hoarse. Then he dropped onto Brett's couch and used the remote to switch on the TV.

Brett narrowed his eyes and stared at his friend. "You okay, bud?''

Carlo stared at the TV screen and grunted again.

That was answer enough for Brett. For some reason, Carlo's habitual good humor had slipped away, and it didn't look like he was going to explain why. Brett shrugged. He had his own share of dark moods and didn't talk much about what bothered him either.

None of which shed light on the bet with Franny.

Hell, why did it bother him? She was two times older than his last memory of her at twelve. And even though he'd only caught a glimpse beneath that dark-brimmed hat she wore, she was doubtless a grown woman. He didn't have one excuse for insinuating himself into her business, unless seeing himself as a kind of brother counted.

And since she had four of the real McCoys already, she could do without him. Anyway, since Patricia's death, he'd steered clear of female entanglements. No sense in compromising his self-made vow now.

Even with someone he merely regarded as a little sister.

THE TWILIGHT AIR smelled of pork roast and potatoes when Brett encountered Franny in the apartment complex's parking lot. She clutched some shopping bags to her body and the handles of others ringed her arms from wrists to elbows. Her hat shaded her eyes again.

A brother would have let a sister struggle onward by herself.

Brett divested her of what he could.

A small smile crossed her face and gleamed in the near darkness. ''My hero!'' she said lightly, then led the way to her apartment, unlocking the door and flipping on the entry hall light. On a nearby hook, she hung her baseball cap.

Brett halted, blinking. "Franny?" For an instant, he thought he'd followed the wrong woman home.

He could see her clearly now. The dark hair that had been in a ponytail earlier in the day now brushed her shoulders. The stuff's shine was so glossy he thought maybe he could see his reflection. More glossiness, wispy layers of it, framed a face that was so like he remembered—and yet so different.

Her half smile faltered. "It's me. A new hairstyle today, but me."

But it wasn't. The Franny that Brett held in his memory had been a little squirt with big dark eyes and a baby nose. This Franny—Francesca—still had the big dark eyes. She still had the cute little nose. But now she had cheekbones and warm golden skin and a mouth with full, lush lips that looked ripe and ready for kissing.

Damn. He stood there, arms full of packages, and couldn't think of one rational thing to say.

She saved him by turning away and leading him toward the living room. He preferred this view of her. In loose jeans and a T-shirt she looked like the girl he remembered.

She threw him a quick look over her shoulder and cleared her throat. "I never really welcomed you back today, did I?"

No, she'd hightailed it out of her father's kitchen nearly the moment he'd entered it. "You said you had someplace to go."

She gestured toward an easy chair and he dropped the bags he'd been carrying onto its seat.

"I had some work to do," she said. "Shopping."

He almost smiled. Few women would think of shopping as "work." Then he figured she was working on winning that bet.

He didn't like how that bothered him. Hadn't he decided not to get involved? "I better head out," he said abruptly, taking a step toward the front door.

His quick movement upset the pile of packages on the easy chair. A wide-mouthed shopping bag slid off the top, spilling several tissue-wrapped items and a small box onto the floor.

They both bent to gather them up. She looked at him over the disarray of clothes, a little smile playing over that brand-new mouth of hers. "Remember the time you took me to the mall?"

And suddenly he did. She'd wanted something new to wear to her first sixth-grade dance. Her brothers had groaned and moaned until Brett had volunteered to give her a ride. And then somehow she'd coerced him into actually *shopping,* in claustrophobia-inducing stores that smelled like bubblegum and hairspray. What a sucker he'd been for her.

Now she stood, rubbing her hands against her pants in a nervous gesture. "Do you, uh, have something important to do right now?"

Caution made him shuffle back a step. "I need to go. I'm supposed to—" Looking into her big brown eyes, he couldn't think of anything he was supposed to do except continue looking.

Her eyebrows rose toward her fringe of bangs. "Really? Darn. I was hoping I could show you what I bought today. Get your opinion. I made a major dent in my credit card and I'm a little nervous about it."

Brett nearly groaned. He was supposed to be keeping his distance. "Why me?"

She smiled. "Because you're perfect. An interested, disinterested party."

He shook his head as if to clear it. "What's that mean, exactly?"

"That I can persuade you to stay, and when I ask if you like something, no matter what you think you'll say yes." That smile of hers widened into a grin.

Something hot shot through Brett. "Maybe I should get Carlo." For both their sakes. "Or Nicky. I think he's still at your dad's. Or all three of them."

Franny frowned. "If even one of the men in my family had an ounce of good taste, do you think I'd look like this?"

She held her arms away from her body, and as instructed, Brett looked. As he'd noticed before, she wore jeans and a T-shirt.

"What? You look fine." He tried to find an apt word. "Useful."

"Useful," she repeated. She turned her back and began restacking her purchases. "Like I could change a tire if I had to?"

She was pretty small for torquing lug nuts off a hub, but he didn't want to insult her. "Ready to go bowling, maybe."

She groaned. "That bad?"

Brett realized he'd said something wrong. Franny must not like to bowl anymore, though she'd gone dozens of times with them when she was a kid. "A tire," he said hastily. "You look like you could definitely change a tire."

Franny sighed. "I think I'm convinced every penny was worth it."

Though he hadn't wanted to get involved, he hadn't wanted to hurt her feelings, either. "I'll go now," he said, taking a few more steps back.

She was already unwrapping the tissue from the first item on the stack. With a flick of her wrist, something skimpy and soft unfurled. Before he made it to the doorway, she turned and held it up against her. "What do you think of this?"

He froze. Plastered against Franny's body was a sleeveless sweater of some sort of soft rose-colored knit fabric.

"Cashmere," she said. "Do you like the color?"

It matched the color in her cheeks, and her lips were shaded just one tone darker. She pressed her palm against her stomach, pinning the little thing even closer to her form, showing the sweet curve of her breasts and accenting the slimness of her waist.

Franny had a top half that was two handfuls of temptation.

Brett immediately wanted to kick himself. This was *Franny*. He regarded her as a *sister*.

Not anymore, a little devil inside him whispered.

Yes, he insisted in return. After Patricia's death he wasn't in the running for anything else.

Franny must have taken his silence as approval, because she started dropping bags to the floor and tossing new clothes across the couch. Short skirts and tight tops in a rainbow of pinks and blues.

The last bag floated to the floor. "Well?" she said.

Well, he wished he'd left twenty minutes ago.

"Wait! Wait! Don't say anything yet!" She dug through one last bag to pull out a perfume atomizer. One spritz filled the room with a scent that was light but seductive. Spicy and sweet. He imagined it warmed by Franny's smooth skin.

"What do you think? As a man, I mean? Does it, uh, entice you?"

"Entice *me?*" The thought had a dangerous appeal.

She flushed. "Not you, of course. I didn't mean—I'm sorry if that offended you. I know that Patricia's death— that you—"

"It's okay."

The color on her cheeks receded. "What I'm asking is what you think. I'm usually a jeans-and-sweatshirt kind of woman. Will I look good in this stuff?"

He knew she was really asking if, wearing it, she'd

find a man—some man who could win her that bet. And after what must be major wear and tear to her credit card's magnetic strip, she probably hadn't enough left to come up with Carlo's hundred bucks. Still, Brett didn't like the idea of Franny shedding her jeans and putting on a skirt for anyone but—

For *anyone*.

The whole thing was none of his business, though.

And sure, Carlo was a jerk for pulling the stunt, but Franny looked more than a little excited by the whole bet idea.

He didn't like that, either.

"Well?" she said impatiently. "Give it to me straight."

He shook his head, eyeing the cavalcade of sexiness strewn across the couch cushions. "I'm just sorry for whoever you unleash this on."

Her smile was brilliant. "Thank you, Brett. Thank you." Her expression turned impish. "You can witness it for yourself tomorrow night."

Oh, no. The last thing he wanted to do was that. He was staying out of the Milano family business. Franny's business.

"We're going out together. Carlo, Nicky, all of us. David Lee and Elise, too."

She would have her brothers there to watch over her. "I don't think—"

"I'm going to wear this." She plucked a skimpy, stretchy dress out of the pile. It was violet. Something that winked like stars dotted the fabric. The short skirt swung as she held it up.

Of course, it had been one of her brothers who had started this whole, dangerous mess. "Tomorrow night I—"

"Haven't another thing to do. Come on. It'll be good for you to go out, Brett."

"N—"

She touched his arm. He couldn't think for a moment. It had been so long since a woman had touched him. More than eighteen months and four days.

"Come with me," Franny said.

She should have said "us," he thought. Then he could have refused. But the "me" made him think of her out alone at night in the violet-and-stars dress that would mold her breasts and swish around her thighs.

"Yes," he said.

2

STALLED by the large crowd filtering through the entry to the country club's banquet room, Francesca tried to separate the notes of the light rock pouring out the door from those of the country band playing on a nearby patio. Then the logjam ahead broke up and she followed the rest of her group inside. The charity fund-raiser—sponsored by two radio stations and some local businesses including the accounting firm Elise's David worked for—was packed, and Francesca was instantly separated from the others. On tiptoe to see over the shoulders of those around her, she finally located her brothers Nicky and Joe, who had already commandeered a couple of tables for the eight in their party.

Francesca skirted the dance floor and took the last seat available, squeezing herself in between Brett and Carlo. Judging by their stiff expressions, they weren't going to be the cheeriest of table mates.

She sighed. Carlo's mood mystified her, but she took some responsibility for Brett's. From all reports, he continued to deeply mourn his fiancée and longtime love, Patricia, who had died so tragically. Maybe twisting his arm to come along tonight hadn't been such a good idea.

Elise's fiancé, David, and Nicky were grousing about the lack of cocktail waitresses. From the other table Elise sent Francesca a significant look and then rolled her eyes in the direction of a group of men by the bar that was set up on the other side of the room.

Right. She wasn't here to fix Brett, but to fix herself up with a man who could win her that bet at the end of the month.

Elise had suggested going to this event as a way to launch Francesca into circulation. In case she felt insecure wearing a new dress, makeup and high heels, she had family and friends as a comfortable homebase. Leaning forward, Francesca put her elbow on the table and her chin in her hand to survey the guys Elise had pointed out.

The right age and not drunk. Two excellent starting points.

"Can I get you something to drink?" Brett's voice made her start. "We've given up on the waitress."

"Oh, um, sure. A glass of red wine would be great," Francesca said, reaching for her purse.

Brett grinned, his sudden smile startling her. "Don't worry about it. Carlo's buying."

She smiled back as both men stood. Carlo had a list of drink orders scribbled on a crumpled cocktail napkin.

Brett followed Carlo, and Francesca peered through the crowd to watch the two as they waited at the bar. Carlo had the dark Italian good looks shared by all the Milano brothers, a handsomeness completely familiar to

Francesca. But Brett was like a different species. He was over six feet, lean and hard looking. His hair was dark blond, his face high-cheekboned. He wore soft jeans and a short-sleeved sports shirt. Its searing color matched the Scandinavian blue of his eyes.

"Mooning over somebody already?" Elise had slipped into the seat vacated by Carlo. "Which one?"

"The least likely candi*date*," Francesca murmured.

"Huh?" Elise leaned closer. "Who?"

Francesca decided against confessing. "I'm not mooning, I'm moaning. *Pantyhose.*"

The return of Carlo and Brett spared Francesca any more probing. After ordering her to "Get to work," Elise returned to her fiancé. Francesca nodded and obediently shifted her attention to the single men beyond the confines of their tables.

It took half a glass of wine to realize she had something else to moan about, though. As one of only two women with six guys, and wedged between the two most forbidding, Francesca realized single men didn't seem much inclined to approach her.

The chairs were half-mooned around the tables to face the band. When her brother Nicky left his seat to grab another beer, Francesca squeezed out of her chair and took Nicky's. At one end of the moon shape, Nicky's spot put her closer to the dance floor and without anyone on her left. Two tables away, a cute guy in khaki pants caught her eye. A thrill zinged through Francesca. She smiled quickly then looked away, hoping he'd come over to chat or ask her to dance.

Maybe this finding a date stuff wasn't so hard!

She focused on her wineglass, but from the corner of her eye kept tabs on Khaki Pants. He pushed out his chair and slowly stood. Francesca's heart started beating faster. And faster, when his tasseled loafers turned in her direction.

Should she look up? Smile? Pretend she didn't see him until he was right in front of her?

"Here you go, Brett." Nicky had returned, a beer in each hand. Brett rose to take the beer and they remained standing on either side of her, hovering like skyscrapers blocking the sun. Between their imposing bodies, Francesca caught sight of the tasseled loafers turning away.

Nicky bent down. "I think I just saved you from dancing with a dweeb. A guy was heading in this direction."

Francesca glared at him. "I can say no to my own dweebs, thank you very much."

Nicky blinked. "Not on my watch, little sister."

Francesca frowned and thought she saw satisfaction cross Brett's face. Certainly that was a thumb's-up Joe sent Nicky's way.

Francesca gritted her teeth. Her brothers' interference was a problem she hadn't anticipated. But they were not going to cause her to lose this bet or this chance to get a life. Catching sight of Khaki Pants in line at the bar, Francesca left the table and determinedly headed that way herself. She would order a diet cola and hope for a chance to speak to the potential dwee—date.

As she threaded through the tables, the headline band was introduced and the audience went from rockin' to raucous. A pulsing bass line buzzed through the soles of her feet, and a renewed determination infused Francesca. She wanted to dance with Khaki.

The bartender filled her order and she moved close to the dance floor, sipping her drink. Her gaze slid toward Khaki Pants, and he smiled at her. Heart starting to flutter, she smiled back. He sidled closer. The band was so loud he'd have to get very close to begin a conversation.

He was still three steps away when her brothers Joe and Tony pounced. Joe took her glass from her hand. Tony pulled her onto the dance floor and immediately spun her to the corner farthest from Khaki. Francesca gave the stranger a mournful, squiggly fingered farewell. He'd already turned away.

When the dance ended, Tony linked his arm with hers and dragged her back to their tables. "I'm not fifteen, Tony," she said through clenched teeth. "Cut me some slack."

Tony pretended he didn't hear and from somewhere dredged up enough gentlemanly manners to pull out a chair and insert her at the table—once again between Carlo and Brett.

If weeping wouldn't have run her brand-new mascara, Francesca might have resorted to it.

Instead, she stared morosely at her half-full glass of

wine and barely touched cola. She might as well give up and go home. Once out of the stretchy knit dress and into comfy sweats, she'd pop a satisfying bag of Orville's finest in her microwave.

Of course, her habit of doing that had led her to this very, dateless moment.

Irritation rose, and she glanced around at her handsome and complacent siblings. Maybe she should just tell her brothers to lay off!

Right. If they listened to her, Joe wouldn't have bought his last girlfriend a car tune-up for Christmas, and Tony wouldn't be permanently tattooed with the name of the woman he'd loved, then lost.

Then there was the possibility of enlisting their help.

She sighed. As if that wouldn't be a total disaster. Consider the one mushy Valentine she'd received in the third grade. Her brothers' idea of fostering a budding romance had been to glower at poor Wesley Burdett for two months and to tease her unmercifully for two *years*.

Only Brett had been able to shut them—

Brett.

Beside her, his beer hit the tabletop with a *clack*. Francesca looked at him—a plan instantly crystallizing.

"I want to dance," she announced loudly across their two tables.

With matching grimaces, her brothers looked at each other expectantly, obviously hoping another would volunteer for sister duty. Only Tony, who had already sacrificed himself, appeared unmoved by her request.

"To *country*," she added.

All four Milano men groaned in pain, as if she'd stated there'd be no cheesecake for Sunday night dessert. They *hated* country music.

Perfect.

She looked over at Brett. "*You* will dance with me, won't you?"

She restrained the smile breaking over her face. He didn't have any choice but to agree, as all four of her brothers sighed with relief, the saps.

Francesca's smile widened. With Brett as escort, she'd make a break for the potential-man-crowded patio where she could conduct her search in sibling-free peace.

A TWINGE OF GUILT pinged Francesca as Brett followed her through the packed room. He probably didn't feel much like dancing, and she'd had no opportunity yet to let him in on her little plan. Of course, she wouldn't tell him the humiliating truth—that she'd made a bet with her big brother to force herself out of the house to look for a man—but she'd make it clear that she only needed his help to escape the overprotective Milanos.

She wasn't expecting him to take her into his arms.

Shivers ran down her spine, a reaction she chalked up to the fresh air breezing through the open door as they neared it.

Once outside in the darkness, Francesca hesitated on the lit pathway that led toward the country-western band.

Another couple brushed by them, hurrying in the direction of the patio. "I love this song," the woman said to the man she tugged along with her. "Come dance with me, honey. Hold me."

Francesca didn't move.

"You okay?" Behind her, Brett's voice tickled her nerve endings.

She remained still, frozen by a thought that was adolescent and silly and about as likely to happen as a twelve-year-old's romantic daydream about an older boy.

If Brett danced with her, if he held her…if he even touched her…she might stop breathing.

The certainty of the thought was scary. It was as if it had been simmering in the back of her mind since the moment he'd entered her father's kitchen yesterday.

She couldn't risk going toward the dance floor just yet.

To the *clickety-clack* of her new high heels, she rushed in the opposite direction of the patio and the country band and stumbled upon a small courtyard surrounded by rose bushes and low trees strung with white fairy lights. At the center she halted beside a sundial set on a waist-high pedestal.

Brett had followed her. "Franny?" His voice was puzzled.

As she turned to face him, the breeze blew, rustling up a faint scent of roses and chilling Francesca's stockinged legs. Her short dress ruffled against her thighs.

Any notion of giving him some vague excuse for not

wanting to dance with him or of making a lame joke about her two left feet evaporated. Brett was staring at her legs. And then his gaze moved up, over her body, a man's gaze of appreciation.

Goose bumps sped over her skin, fast as a kid with a baseball mitt running away from a broken window.

From between his teeth came the sound of a light, sweet wolf whistle and he shook his head slowly. "Franny—no—*Francesca*. What happened to you? Where'd you go?"

She couldn't think of anything to say.

He moved closer and she retreated, the small of her back pressed against the pedestal. "You've been in my head all these years," he said. "A little urchin with brown eyes and a stubborn chin." He shook his head again. "You weren't supposed to change."

Another spurt of breeze blew by, flattening her dress against her body. "You've been gone a long time, Brett." She swallowed, trying to ease the croak in her voice.

"That long?"

She swallowed again. "Long enough for me to grow up."

He was silent a minute, then he laughed ruefully. "Doesn't seem like your brothers have accepted that."

"No," she agreed.

"So then why should I?"

She stared at her feet, unfamiliar in their pointy-toed high heels. *Because I want you to see me as a woman.*

Her teeth came down on her tongue to stop the silly, adolescent-daydream words.

"Francesca…"

He was moving closer again, and she tried to move back, but one of her heels caught on the pedestal base behind her and she lost her balance. Brett made like he was going to catch her and, desperate to keep free of his touch, she twisted, her hand grabbing the metal pointer of the sundial to keep herself upright.

It bit sharply into her hand. "Ouch!"

"What happened?" He reached for her fingers, but she whirled away in time.

"Nothing. Just a little cut." And a large dose of embarrassment, she thought. See her as a woman? Brett was seeing her as a klutz.

"Let's go get some disinfectant for that."

"No way!" Francesca made a wide circle around him and headed toward the main path. "I hate the stuff. Stings like the dickens. I'll run water over it in the ladies' room."

He was following her again and she avoided looking at him by walking briskly to remain in the lead.

His voice stopped her outside a door marked Women. "Francesca," he said.

"Yes?" She swung around slowly.

Fairy lights were strung in the trees here, too, and they backlit Brett, dazzling her. "You grew up beautiful," he said.

Her knees melted. The throbbing of her cut hand suddenly triple-timed to match the startled beating of her heart. And Francesca realized it took less than Brett's touch to rob her of air.

ON THE LARGE PATIO hosting the country-western band, Brett kept an eye on Francesca from a table placed deep in the shadows of bordering shrubbery. He nursed a beer, his gaze not leaving her as she attempted the intricate steps of a line dance.

She turned the wrong way, laughed, then pushed that gleaming hair of hers out of her eyes. In the dimly lit dance area, the stars on her dress winked like a thousand shiny enticements.

Just as he'd imagined the evening before, the dress displayed her body in a way that boyish jeans and over-size T-shirts couldn't. Rounded and slender in all the right places, Francesca was built like a womanly gymnast—taut muscles and full breasts.

As if responding to his thought, two men moved from another line to take up places beside her. Brett gripped his beer hard.

He was going to keep his distance.

After she'd tended to her hand—he'd scrounged a bandage from the club personnel—she'd avoided his gaze while telling him she didn't want that dance after all. Her reasons had been less than clear, but he'd let her off the hook without a fight.

Though she didn't know it, he was aware of her bet

with Carlo. She was looking for a hot prospect and needed freedom from her brothers to accomplish it.

But not freedom from him.

No, he'd assigned himself the task of watching over her for the evening. Any man who was going to get Francesca was going to have to pass muster with him first.

One of the men beside her bent toward her ear. She looked up at him and smiled, her eyes shadowed and mysterious. The ends of her smooth dark hair brushed against her star-strewn dress, and now the second man leaned toward her.

Brett's gut burned. Damn. She was innocent and gorgeous and he wanted to keep her safe.

"Hi." In front of him, a feminine voice intruded. A tall blonde slid onto the chair opposite him. "Taken?"

He shook his head. From the corner of his eye, he checked out Francesca again. Flanked by the two men, she was still gamely attempting the dance.

"Having a good time tonight?" The blonde's long fall of hair reminded him of Patricia.

His insides twisted, but he forced out a brief smile. "Sure."

"I just got dumped," the woman said. The last half of her glass—the olived toothpick made it look like a martini—went down in one gulp.

The big-beat country song ended and Francesca was clapping. So were the men beside her, both smiling down at her.

Brett glued his gaze on them. The blonde beside him was still talking.

"He was a rat, but a generous rat. You know. Flowers. Jewelry." Her other ringed hand moved, and Brett realized she held a second drink. Her black, highly arched eyebrows rose. "You want one?" She gestured toward her glass. "Vodka martini."

"No, thanks." The first guy who had spoken to Francesca, long haired and tight jeaned, bent close. Brett kept his eyes on him as Francesca nodded, then smiled another time.

"As I was saying." The blonde across from him again. "He really had me going. He said all the right words. Made all the right moves. Gave me a *diamond*."

Brett kept his mouth shut. He couldn't believe this lady was confiding in him. He'd never been the girl's-best-friend type.

Francesca did another smile-nod-smile as the long-haired one leaned toward her and talked.

The woman beside Brett downed her next martini in two gulps, and he figured it was the vodka and vermouth that had chosen him as her confidant. "So tell me," she said, her voice insistent. "You're a man. Why would he do it?"

Brett stared at the blonde. Men *did* disappoint women. That guy could do a number on Francesca. Some other man she met tonight might break her heart.

Could? Might? *Hah!* It was practically a certainty.

God and he knew life didn't run smoothly, even if you had beauty and youth on your side.

The thought panicked him. He glanced over to check on Francesca. The long-haired man bent even nearer her ear. More smiles were exchanged.

Brett's hand tightened on his sweating bottle of beer. The band hadn't started their next song, so the patio wasn't noisy enough to warrant the other man's closeness.

"Who's she?" With a three-olive toothpick, the blonde gestured toward the dance area. "The woman you can't keep your eyes off."

"A friend." How annoyed would Francesca be if he wandered over?

She laughed. "Yeah, and the rat's going to give up his cheese and come back to me."

It was Francesca who was laughing now. She put her hand on the sleeve of the guy talking with her. He grinned and covered her fingers with his.

Brett stood. He would just introduce himself. Let this potential rat know that Francesca had people looking out for her. Just as he took a step forward, the rat gave Francesca a two-fingered salute and strode away. The other man who'd been hanging by her trailed behind.

Brett could relax now. Could resume his seat across from the blonde and take her drunken meandering as a reminder of how risky love was.

Or...

He could take a step forward in a suddenly formed

plan he had for Francesca. The one where it was he who helped her win Carlo's bet.

Why not? For her pride, or the money or both, Francesca was determined to win that bet by the day of Elise and David's wedding. But that deadline could lead a naive young woman to trouble or pain.

The band started up something slow and country. Brett imagined Francesca in the long-haired rat's embrace, his big hands on her body.

Brett found himself striding toward her. Standing at the edge of the dance floor, she didn't see him coming. He grabbed that hand that had been touching the rat and pulled her into the circle of dancers.

Then he pulled her into the circle of his arms.

God. Her dark and grown-up eyes stared up at him, and he wanted to answer all the questions they asked.

He'd say anything to make her smile.

"You looked…" As if she could be hurt on this man-hunt. As if he could step in like he'd done all those years ago and make everything better.

And then he stopped thinking and started registering how Francesca felt in his embrace. He took in a deep breath and that perfume she'd tested on him the night before entered his lungs.

His body hardened.

It didn't surprise him. Over a year and a half had passed since he'd held a woman. But he didn't want to scare Francesca by a purely natural reawakening of physical response, so he edged away from her.

It seemed to him she sighed.

Keeping her inches away, he shuffled his feet to the slow beat of the music.

He took in another breath of that sweet and spicy perfume. It joined with another warm scent—her skin, he guessed—and suddenly his head dizzied with the mix of the fragrance and the flashing stars on her spangly dress.

"Francesca." Like a man with handfuls of unexpected treasure, he stared down at her, amazed.

She looked up, her eyes going wide at what she saw on his face. And what *did* she see? Arousal, surprise, that odd resurgence of the all's-right-with-the-world feeling?

His hand rested on her shoulder and the soft ends of her hair slid across his knuckles, sending more sparklers of sensation up his arm.

"Why are you doing this, Brett?" she asked.

Dancing? Feeling? "Because I want to take you out," he answered. "What do you say?"

3

ELISE PULLED a paper napkin from the dispenser on Francesca's kitchen table and wiped her hands free of sandwich crumbs. "Well," Elise said impatiently. "What *did* you say?"

Francesca gathered up their plates and turned toward the sink. "What should I have said?"

"Francesca…"

"Okay, okay." Francesca surrendered the secret she'd been hugging to herself for the past fifteen hours. "When Brett asked me if I'd go out, I said yes."

Elise stared at her, her chin sagging in obvious surprise. "Francesca Milano dating Brett Swenson?"

Maybe she should take her best friend's disbelief as an insult, but to be honest, Francesca had been just as startled by the notion herself. "It sort of popped out of my mouth," she explained. "My head was thinking 'no way,' but my—"

"Good sense must have gone to Tahiti!"

"Elise…"

"Francesca…" Elise sank back in her chair in an attitude of despair. "You've got to know better than this."

With quick movements, Francesca loaded her dishwasher. Yes, she'd known the idea of tomboy Francesca on a date with gorgeous Brett Swenson bordered on the impossible, but she'd been dizzied. Those fairy lights. The intensity of Brett's blue eyes. The strength of his arms around her and the almost painful flutter of her heart when his hands had brushed her skin.

She'd thought if he touched her she'd lose her breath. Instead she'd lost her head.

Swallowing, she turned toward Elise slowly. "I know it's like the peacock and the mud hen, but…"

Elise shook her head. "That's not what I mean at all!" Frowning, she jabbed her finger in Francesca's direction. "You keep forgetting to look in the mirror."

"But—"

"But nothing. Brett Swenson or any man would be lucky to have you. Problem is, Brett Swenson isn't looking to have anyone."

Now why should those words make her ache? "I know," Francesca answered honestly. "But he did ask."

Elise worried her lower lip. "Which bothers me. But I *am* glad you're under no delusions."

Not delusional. Not even hopeful. Just… "I know I could have refused." It had even crossed her mind for half a millisecond.

"But?" Elise prompted. "Because you also know you shouldn't be wasting your time with nonpotentials."

Right. There was that bet at the end of the month. Her

need to win the guy gamble. And that other need she had, deep inside, to finally, finally fall in love.

"But—" Francesca didn't know the reason she'd agreed herself, so she tried making it up as she went along. "But maybe I figured we both needed an easing-in."

Elise raised her blond eyebrows in perfect arches.

Francesca felt the beginnings of a cold sweat. "Hey, with my dismal dating scorecard, I could use the practice," she said quickly. "And Brett, maybe Brett wants to dip a toe back into the dating pool."

Elise crossed her arms over her chest. "As long as it's just a toe."

"C'mon." Francesca smiled. "I have four brothers singing that song. Just be happy I'm going out instead of sitting at home with my cat and reruns of 'Happy Days.'"

Her best friend rubbed a crimson-tipped finger over her nose. "You are pretty pitiful."

"See? Now help me find something to wear tonight."

Clapping her hands together, Elise popped out of the chair. "Oh! Closet combing. My favorite. Where's he taking you?"

Francesca stopped herself in the act of biting off her thumbnail. "He left it up to me. I chose the fun center."

Elise looked ready for another heart attack. "The fun center? Pee-wee golf? Bumper boats? Those machines that go ding-ding-ding? That kind of fun center?"

"Pinball machines, Elise. And yes, that kind of fun

center.'' Francesca braced herself for her friend's next explosion at her unconventional choice.

"Whew." Wiping her brow dramatically, Elise dropped back to the seat of her chair. ''You should have told me that in the first place. I can't tell you how relieved I am.''

It was Francesca's turn for bewilderment. ''Huh?''

''Sweetie,'' Elise said. ''You had me worried for a bit there, about Brett breaking your heart. But you are a smart girl.''

Francesca was really glad to hear that, of course, but she couldn't suppress her second ''Huh?''

''The fun center's no date,'' Elise proclaimed. ''That's just a boys' night out.''

BOYS' NIGHT OUT. Elise's comment echoed as Francesca stared at her reflection. With a tiny groan of regret she pulled off her baseball cap and tossed it on the bed. Jeans, tennies and an ''I Stop For Roadkill'' sweatshirt were statement enough.

The statement being: Boys' night out.

Because the minute Elise said it and the more Francesca thought about it, that was probably what Brett meant to suggest anyway. Yeah, yeah, he'd said she'd ''grown up beautiful'' and all, but that didn't guarantee he'd asked her out on a *date* date.

Heck, the poor man was new to town and lived just a few doors down. He probably wanted company. He'd probably tried Nicky, Tony, Joe and Carlo first. Pop even. But Tuesday nights the men in her family all had commitments—jaycee meetings, basketball leagues, Pop hit the bingo game down at the local church and always took at least one of her brothers and three or four of their senior residents with him.

Only Francesca had been available to "date" tonight.

Good thing she'd suggested the fun center—the first thing that had popped into her mind—instead of a dead giveaway like an ocean-view restaurant or a picnic bonfire on the beach.

Yeah, she and Brett, just two good buddies, were going to spend the evening playing games.

Kid games, not man-woman games.

And in her tennies, second-best jeans and the sweatshirt Nicky had given her for Christmas, she'd make clear she understood her good-friend, just-one-of-the-boys status. Thinking again, she made a grab for the ball cap. An additional reminder wasn't a bad idea.

Tugging it over her hair, she looked straight into her reflected gaze and vowed not to make the mistake of considering this a real date.

Then the doorbell rang. With a final deep breath, she jogged toward her front door and pulled it open as she pasted on her best and friendliest smile.

To feel it slide right from her lips.

She tried resurrecting it, she honestly did, but Brett looked so *good*.

Feet in suede hikers, long legs in denim, then a soft

yellow sports shirt. Her gaze traveled upward, taking in his wide grin and Scandinavian eyes.

Young Italian women must be susceptible to blue.

With effort, she curved up the corners of her mouth. "Hey, pal." *Friends. One of the boys.*

His eyes laughed a little. "Back at ya."

On the way to the parking lot they easily dispensed with the how-was-your-day stuff. At his Jeep, though, she was startled to find herself wrestling with him for the door handle.

On her side. The passenger side.

It took a moment to realize he was opening the door for her. Like a real, honest-to-goodness date.

She swallowed. "Oh, you don't—"

"I do." Brett put his hand beneath her elbow to boost her into the high seat.

As he shut the door and circled to his side, Francesca rubbed at the goose bumps on her arms and tried to think. Something wasn't quite right here.

Too soon, he was behind the steering wheel. In the closed confines of the car Francesca breathed in his scent, just a hint of citrusy soap. Her brothers all used something orange and antibacterial that made them smell…sanitized. Closing her eyes, she sniffed again in appreciation.

"Francesca?"

She snapped to attention to find Brett looking at her expectantly.

She stared back, mystified. What had she forgotten? "Uh," she responded, exhibiting her high IQ.

Brett grinned, then reached across her for the shoulder harness. He buckled her in like he would a child…or a woman.

"Uh," she said again.

He raised his eyebrows.

Opening the car door for her, helping her into her seat, buckling the seat belt. She couldn't see Brett doing those things for Carlo. Not considerations you'd give to one of the boys. Or if you did, one of the boys might just slug you.

She licked her lips, wondering where she'd gone wrong. *Was* this a date? Clearing her throat, she tentatively tested the theory.

"I guess," she started, then cleared her throat again. "I guess you know that my brothers are all busy tonight."

If he could catalog their activities, she would know he'd asked them out first.

His sandy eyebrows came together, and a gleam entered his eyes. "Francesca." His tone was mildly shocked and mostly amused. "You're not trying to tell me no one will be waiting up for you tonight, are you?"

Francesca nearly swallowed her tongue. "No! Yes!" Those double negative questions always tripped her up. "I didn't mean anything by it." Her cheeks burned. "Nothing at all."

She quickly averted her gaze to his hands, focusing

on his long, capable fingers, which then turned the key to start the car. As the engine vroomed to life, vibrations hummed against her toes, curled tightly against the soles of her shoes.

Her fingers were curled tightly too, meshed with each other in a tense bundle beneath "Roadkill" on her sweatshirt.

Forcing out a long breath of air, she commanded herself to relax. She'd feel better once she knew for sure Brett's expectations for the evening.

He turned out of the parking lot and she tried again to pin down the situation. In a roundabout way, of course. "I think we'll have a good time at the fun center, don't you?" she said brightly.

If he agreed enthusiastically, it signified boys' night out.

He shrugged.

A shrug! What did a shrug mean?

Francesca stifled a groan. Why, oh, why hadn't she made an effort to date before now? With a little more experience she'd be better able to interpret these nuances. One of her hands crept over her eyes.

"Francesca?" He sounded slightly worried. "What's the matter? What're you thinking?"

"That I should be married with three kids." Then the waiting and the wondering would be over. She'd be settled and satisfied and—

Would have missed the chance at Brett Swenson.

"Then we wouldn't be having this date," he said, just as if he could read her mind.

"Is that what this is?" Francesca whispered. "A date?" In her jeans and her tennis shoes and her roadkill sweatshirt she was actually *dating* Brett Swenson?

"What would you call it?"

Something she should have used a curling iron for.

Something that warranted every feminine grace and womanly wile she'd ever heard or read about.

Something she'd wished for on every girlhood star.

A TALK-SHOW ROMANCE GURU insisted that a man enjoyed an evening most when his date made him feel like a king.

Francesca focused on the insight for the entire thirty steps from the car to the fun center entrance. But then an instinct kicked in—a primordial kill-or-be-killed instinct—honed over twenty-four years of being the smallest and youngest, constantly challenged by the older and stronger.

Not just a survival instinct, but a winning instinct.

So, without even thinking, she outscored Brett at pinball. Rammed him unmercifully with her bumper car. Beat him at air hockey.

Not until now, she thought, as she putted into the smiling, red mouth of the clown at the seventeenth and second-to-last hole of the miniature golf course, did Francesca remember her original intention to follow the guru's advice and give Brett the King treatment.

And their scores were tied.

Her cheeks burned in embarrassment as she considered the evening from Brett's point of view. If he'd actually wanted a date, she didn't know *what* she'd given him instead.

"You're suddenly quiet," he said as they waited for the group in front of them to finish the eighteenth hole. "Thinking of the old place?"

Suddenly quiet? Thinking of the old place? She wanted to bury her head in her hands. In between her triumphant exclaims of "Gotcha!" and promises like "I'm gonna whup you now!" she'd told Brett nearly every detail of her life—including the family decision to sell their childhood home and move into a set of apartments.

He gave a gentle tug to the end of her ponytail escaping from her ball cap. "Some memories are hard to let go of."

Great. Now she had him thinking of Patricia, the golden-haired beauty who had known how to date, how to talk to a man, how to make him feel like a king.

On the eighteenth "green" of indoor-outdoor carpeting, Brett let Francesca tee off first. The end of the hole was around a bend, and a good player would ricochet her ball off the dead end curb in front of her to send it toward the putting area. Instead, Francesca let loose a weak swing that caused the ball to stutter unremarkably down the pee-wee fairway.

He gave her a considering look, then stepped up and

made the shot that she'd wanted to. Because his ball was closest to the hole, he had to wait while she took two more ineffectual swings to get her ball within range.

Using the stubby pencil, Francesca kept track of her strokes with hash marks. Pursing her lips, she glued her gaze to the scorecard. "You're obviously the superior player," she said. "I don't have a chance."

He threw her another odd glance but didn't say anything, even as she struggled to make sure her ball hit the red revolving door of the miniature schoolhouse three times before letting it finally make it through to settle into the cup.

Brett made it in one.

She threw up her hands. "The winner!" she said. *The king.* Hoping she'd gotten this date thing right—better late than never—she smiled at him.

He didn't smile back.

Instead, he grabbed her hand and tugged her to the car. After opening her door and helping her in, he drove the short way home in silence.

BRETT PULLED into the last stall in the apartment parking lot. He turned off the car but kept his hands on the wheel, determined not to use them to throttle Francesca.

She cleared her throat nervously. "The security lights don't reach this space well. I'll have to do something about that."

"Tomorrow," Brett answered shortly. "I like the darkness now."

"You do?"

"I chose it for a reason."

"You did?"

"Because if you could see my face, Francesca, I'd scare you."

A hint of guilt crept into her voice. "You saw the mustard stain on your shirt? I'm really sorry. That corndog—"

"No." He was so mad he couldn't think clearly. And his anger was all muddled by the image of unholy and gorgeous glee on her face as she rammed him with her bumper car. Of her spectacular wins at air hockey and the little sizzle sound she'd made with her tongue against her teeth after licking her forefinger and then touching her skin.

"I'm hot," she'd said.

By God, she was, and so was the image of her cute little tush bent over the pinball machine. The memory burned a hole in his brain.

But then—

"Damn it, Francesca! Why'd you go all soft on me?" He couldn't restrain his irritation.

"I…I don't know what you mean," she said hesitantly.

"But you do. Admit it. You let me win at miniature golf."

Even in the darkness he could tell she squirmed on her seat. "No. You were just better—"

"I was *maybe* equal."

She tried again. "You can't know—"

"I know."

She sagged against the seatback.

He wasn't going to let her off the hook. "Why, Francesca?"

"I—" She lifted her hand, let it drop to her thigh. He heard her sigh. "You said it yourself. I wanted to go soft on you."

"To what purpose?"

"I don't know." She sighed again. "To make you feel like a king. To show you a good time. To be a real date."

Something inside Brett twisted into pretzel knots. Damn. She was a walking romantic tragedy just waiting to happen.

Another wave of anger rose. "Hell, Francesca. Tell me you know *not* to be showing guys a 'good time.' Tell me your brothers have taught you better than to make some man feel like a king." He was working up a real mood to kick some Milano-men butt.

Her head hit the back of the seat with a muted thud. "That's the whole problem! They've only taught me to how to *win* and nothing about how to *date*."

He thought he just might lose it. His hands started to shake and he gripped the steering wheel to stop them. *Thank God.* Thank God and the blasted universe that she hadn't made this nutty bet with Carlo months ago. Who would have protected her then?

"Francesca," he said, not surprised at all to find his voice hoarse. "What am I going to do with you?"

The little bit of laughter in *her* voice surprised him, though. "Not beat me at miniature golf next time?"

That pretzel knot inside him twisted tighter. He swallowed. "Exactly. Francesca, don't change *anything* about yourself when you're with a man, okay? Promise me?"

"Even my habit of dripping mustard?" She was trying to keep it light.

"Even that. Men don't care about mustard stains."

"Ain't that the truth." She sat up straight and swiveled his way. "I've lived with four brothers, remember?"

"I remember." And those four brothers and one loving father had created the female before him. An incredible mix of naïveté and beauty and go-for-it guts.

"Francesca." He said her name just because it rolled so sweetly off his tongue, and he let go of the steering wheel.

"I wanted tonight to be perfect," she said, a mournful note in her voice.

He smiled. With his forefinger, he reached out and traced the brim of her ballcap. "It was perfect. Seriously. I haven't had a good time like that in a long while. The 'Roadkill' sweatshirt capped it off for me."

She groaned. "Don't blame me. This was Nicky's Christmas gift."

"What? No perfume? No fuzzy sweaters for his little sister?"

She shook her head. "Nope. And the others gave me sweatsocks and cookbooks."

Something made him probe a little further. "No boy-friend to give you lacy naughty stuff?"

"Me?" A shocked, very feminine giggle floated through the car. "Who could imagine me in lacy and naughty?"

He could. The idea fired his blood to red-lace-teddy temperature. He gritted his teeth against the *bam-bam-bam* of his heating pulse.

"We should probably go in," he said tightly. Smart move. Safe move.

"Right." She hesitated. "Right."

Damn. He could read her hesitation in mile-high let-ters. A date should end with a kiss. A perfect date should end with a perfect kiss.

A chaste, first-date kind of kiss and here he was, burn-ing up thinking about her tush and lace teddies.

He ground his molars again. So it had been a long time since he'd been with a woman. That didn't mean he couldn't offer Francesca the kind of good-night that she deserved.

Sweet, warm. A simple thank-you for what had been pure fun and unexpected exhilaration.

"You're going to have to teach me that slick, air-hockey move you have," he said.

"I might," she said with mock haughtiness. "But what's in it for me?"

He smiled slowly. "I have a few moves of my own I could show you."

And then, so that she'd know what he had in mind, he put his forefinger to her hat brim again. He tipped it off her head. It tumbled away, falling against her shoulder and then to the floor of the car.

She bent forward.

"Leave it," he said.

She froze, and he slowly leaned toward her. *Simple. Chaste. Warm.*

His heart slammed against his ribs, like a warning to do this right. *Do it right for Francesca.*

He cupped her cheek with his palm, curling his fingers around her jaw and tilting her mouth up.

His blood was burning now, pounding along with his heartbeat in a steady path to his groin. He closed his eyes against the good ache and tried to think only of Francesca. Of her trust in him.

Simple. Chaste.

He brushed her lips. Like he might a maiden aunt or a little sister or a good friend.

But a teasing hint of her taste tempted him. Leaning closer, he pressed harder against her mouth.

And though he sensed it about to happen, and though he screamed *No!* in his mind, and though he could have moved away himself, he felt her lips part.

Her sweet, heated breath rushed over his lips.

Simple.

Simply nothing could stop him from taking more.

4

FRANCESCA TASTED like cotton candy. The kiss melted on Brett's tongue, pink and sweet. He should stop now. Pull away. But who had the willpower for just one taste of that fluffy stuff?

He pressed closer again, her mouth opened again, and he moved his tongue softly inside. Okay, so he'd have belted any other guy who made such a move on Francesca on a first date, but he couldn't resist. She inhaled a little startled gasp, and he tensed, ready to leave her, then her tongue met his, stroked against it as if she was joyfully discovering a brand new flavor of ice cream.

He went rock hard.

Not trusting himself, he dropped his hand from the golden smoothness of her skin. But on the way down, his fingers brushed her thigh, slender and firm, and he found he couldn't move. He laid his palm there but thought he'd better break the kiss.

He tried, really. But when he moved his tongue from her mouth she chased it into his. The maneuver seduced him. He gripped her thigh and the sound of another of her soft gasps lit a match to an already smoldering sexual burn.

Heat and instinct overtook him. He reclaimed the kiss, sliding into her mouth with a sure stroke and then exploring her teeth, her tongue, the response she made when he set up a thrusting rhythm.

She moaned, twisted to get closer to him, and he found his fingers dangerously close to the heat between her thighs. A hot chill ran up his arm toward his chest. Just millimeters and he could touch Francesca more intimately.

The thought hit him like a slap. Francesca! This was *Francesca* moaning against his mouth. *Francesca's* tense thigh beneath his fingers.

Francesca!

He snatched his hand from her and abruptly lifted away from her mouth. She stared at him, a dazed look on her face. Brett's shoulders and neck tensed.

Any minute now she'd realize what had happened to a simple good-night kiss. Any minute now awkwardness would descend and the dazzle on Francesca's face would disappear.

"Let me walk you to your door," Brett said quickly. Maybe he could get her there before embarrassment changed things between them, before the wetness of his kiss on her lips dried.

Because he wanted to go to bed remembering her just like this. Eyes dark and wide, mouth rosy and wet.

Hell, who needed sleep?

She jumped out of the car before he could make it around to her side. She practically ran to her apartment, pulling her house keys from her pocket even before reaching the door.

Halfway over the threshold, she paused. As she turned around, her hand came up. Maybe she was angry. Maybe she was going to slap him. Oh, he hoped she would.

But her face was unreadable and her palm felt cool as she laid it against his hot cheek. "I had fun, too," she said, then slipped inside and shut the door.

Fun? *Fun?* Brett worried about that term all the way back to his own apartment.

THE NEXT DAY Brett focused on work. He didn't let himself think of anything but briefs, cases and court appearances, and it was a good day. A very good day. Until Carlo Milano showed up in his office. Carlo, Francesca's big brother.

Francesca, whose mouth should come with caution signs.

Carlo peered at him beneath one raised brow. "You with me, Brett? You have time to talk?"

Oh, yeah. He was here as Carlo the police detective. They had business to discuss. Legal business. Unless Carlo was here to talk about Francesca. About how Brett had kissed her so damn silly that he hadn't slept more than forty minutes last night. But he didn't think his best friend would be wearing that faint smile if he had any knowledge of that.

Carlo waved a hand in front of Brett's face. "The

Rearden case? Yesterday you said you had some questions for me?''

Yesterday. Before Francesca's mouth had melted beneath his.

Brett stacked the papers he'd been looking over. ''Right.''

Carlo slouched in the chair across from Brett's desk. ''You okay, bud? You look like you've been flattened by a steamroller.''

Brett grimaced. ''A steamroller.'' Yeah, she'd rolled right over his good intentions.

Shaking his head, Carlo narrowed his eyes. ''A *female* steamroller. I recognize the look.''

Brett wasn't going there with Francesca's brother. ''Huh.'' He grunted noncommittally.

''You can tell me,'' Carlo said.

''Huh.'' Brett grunted again.

''Okay, okay.'' Carlo put up his hands. ''I won't ask anymore. But after Patricia...'' He cleared his throat. ''Didn't you tell me you'd, uh, withdrawn from the fray?''

The fray. Relationships. Love. After Patricia's death Brett had mourned the girl he'd cared about since high school. And though his grieving had ended, he'd decided that he didn't want to involve himself like that again. Too much potential for pain.

''Brett?'' Carlo grimaced. ''Hey, hope I didn't say the wrong thing.''

Brett waved away his friend's concern. "Don't worry about it."

"Then bear with me for another moment here. From what I see on your face I think you need to hear the same advice I've been giving myself."

Brett cocked an eyebrow.

"Lighten up."

"Lighten up?" Brett repeated, wondering what was weighing so heavily on Carlo's mind.

"Yeah. Two words to live by," he said, without adding any more.

"Lighten up." Rubbing his stiff neck, Brett took a moment to try out the concept. Lighten up.

Lighten up. Relief sluiced through him. Hell, he *had* been worried about nothing.

They'd exchanged a kiss. A hot kiss, but still just a kiss. There was no reason to attach any more importance to it. It needn't even change things between him and Francesca. If he kept his mind off her mouth and on winning that bet of hers, he could still help her.

Without anyone getting hurt.

BY THE TIME Brett made his way through the apartment's parking lot that evening, he'd completely expunged the kiss from his mind and was ready to proceed with his bet-winning plan. Busy tucking his cell phone in his pocket and juggling his briefcase, he tripped over Francesca. Literally tripped over her feet, sticking out from beneath her small red-and-white clunker of a pickup truck.

Her "Hey, watch it!" came out slightly muffled and characteristically direct.

He grinned. This Francesca was the same one who had trounced him in air hockey. Tomboy Francesca, who apparently could change oil like a pro, if the stacked quarts of oil beside the truck were any indication. This was the Francesca he could completely control his reaction to.

With the toe of his leather shoe he nudged one of her rubber-thonged feet. "Good evening to you, too."

Her legs stiffened. Not much, but just enough for him to guess she might be thinking about how the night before ended. Which, damn it, started him thinking about how the night before ended, too.

"Oh, hi," she called out.

She was wearing a paint-stained and holey pair of cutoff shorts. Below the fraying hem was the length of her legs. Curved, feminine, slightly tanned. Brett slid his gaze off the sweet line of her calf to focus on the scar on her knee. Ah, now *that* reminded him of the Francesca of the past. Relief again. He smiled.

"Good day?" he asked.

"Fine. Yours?" Her voice still sounded strained. Either she was having trouble unscrewing the oil drain plug or she was uncomfortable around him.

Because of the kiss.

He ignored the thought and shifted his briefcase to the other hand. "Listen. About last night—"

Beneath the car, something clattered to the ground.

"You okay?" he asked hastily.

"Fine! Completely fine!"

He'd planned on saying he'd had fun the night before and then asking her out again. But her voice sounded so odd. If he made her that uneasy, if they couldn't get past that wild burst of passion...

He stared at the bottom half of her, his back teeth grinding in frustration. What was the right thing to do? Retreat? Pursue? Damn, he hated making blind decisions, but he didn't have a clue what she was thinking when all he could see of her was thighs to toes.

"Francesca," he started.

Toes. Suddenly they snagged his attention. He leaned closer. Francesca had painted her toenails. A light pink, but painted all the same. And obviously she was no expert. The color was swiped across the edge of one little toe and smudged on another.

"What?" she said from beneath the truck.

"I—I—" Damn. The innocent and mussed nail polish tugged him so hard and in so many places he could hardly speak.

But he could hardly let her go so some guy could break her heart, either.

"I wondered if you're free for dinner this weekend," he said.

That got him a full look at her. She scooched from

beneath the engine, grease on her T-shirt, the drain plug dripping oil from her fingers to catch on the utilitarian plastic band of her digital watch. Her brown eyes were wide and she had another black streak across one cheek.

He could almost ignore the full rosiness of her mouth.

Yeah. They could go out again. Nobody would get hurt that way.

IN HER father's kitchen, Francesca wiped her palms against the butcher-style apron she wore over her new dress. Carlo breezed in and greedily eyed the pile of croutons that sat ready to garnish the green salad she'd made as part of their Saturday-night dinner of lasagna and garlic bread.

His fingers inched out, and she quickly slapped them back.

"Ow!" He threw her a wounded look. "Can you blame me? Those gotta be homemade. What, does Pop have the bishop on the guest list tonight?"

Francesca shook her head. "Just Pop and the five of us kids." She paused. "And Brett."

"Mmm." Carlo had turned to stick his head in the refrigerator and didn't seem the least perturbed by the news.

No, the "perturb" was all Francesca's and all stemmed from their date…and their kiss.

That kiss.

It should be a constitutional right for a woman to receive at least one kiss like that. A sweet-then-hot kiss from the one man she'd fantasized about her entire life. Some women would pick a movie star or sports celebrity as their fantasy men, but Francesca would choose Brett Swenson every time.

Anytime.

Which was where the whole situation got sticky. She couldn't go on expecting more kisses like that from Brett. Yes, he'd asked her out, then kissed her, then asked her out again. But was it because he was so attracted to her? More likely he'd done all of the above because he was lonely and still reeling from the shock of losing Patricia.

He wanted companionship.

And she'd always wanted him. But it was different now. No longer a twelve-year-old who lived for him to notice her, Francesca was a grown woman who had finally decided to start acting like one.

But though she might be slipping on high heels every once in a while, that didn't mean she'd reached Brett Swenson height. He was still beyond her reach. So when he'd asked her out that second time she'd closed her ears to every passionate impulse that urged her to scream ''Yes!'' and instead invited him to join the family tonight.

Francesca narrowed her gaze at Carlo, who looked like he was about to take a swig straight from the milk carton. Catching her look, he rolled his eyes and grabbed for a glass instead.

You had to be careful around men. Francesca knew

that. And the way she figured it, she'd be safer looking at Brett as just another one of her brothers.

Just another one of her brothers.

She did fine with the decision, all through the greeting him at Pop's front door—his eyes looked laser blue, but she valiantly ignored it—the accepting of the bottle of red wine he'd brought—she made sure his fingers didn't brush hers—and the sitting down to the meal—when to her brothers' astonishment Brett held out a chair to place her at the head of the table opposite her father.

Francesca even looked around with some satisfaction at her family of males—Brett included—as they sighed and grunted and moaned in appreciation over the hot dinner that she tried to provide for them once a week. On her right, Brett offered to serve her some salad, and she managed to see it as a brotherly gesture.

Then Pop broke into the clattering of serving spoons. "Franny, you've still got your apron on."

Automatically Francesca felt behind her for the bow at the small of her back and loosened it. But then she froze as all eyes turned her way. Usually she hated being caught at the dining table still in her apron. But usually she was wearing something equally practical underneath.

Tonight, though, she'd put on a dress that silver-tongued Elise had talked her into. And why she'd chosen tonight of all nights to debut the pink tropical-print thing, she really couldn't say. The men were all still looking at her. Five pairs of brown eyes. One pair of searing blue.

She laughed stiffly. "Oh, maybe I'll just keep—"

Smiling kindly, Brett slipped the apron's top loop over her head.

Six sets of eyebrows rose skyward. Six pairs of eyes focused chest high.

The apron slid from Brett's suddenly slack hand to the floor.

"Franny," somebody said.

Her brother Joe choked on his wine and grabbed desperately for a napkin.

Francesca wished they were kids again and the stuff would spew from his nose, because then everyone would look at Joe instead of her chest.

As it was, their stares compelled her to look down at herself. How bad could it be?

Pretty bad.

Elise had said the dress fit her like a glove. Well, yes. But the spaghetti-strapped, square-necked bodice fit like a glove because it pushed some essential body parts over the top. No more was exposed than any other twenty-something female showed on a regular basis, but it was *tons* more than Francesca had ever revealed.

For years the men in her family had treated her like a pesky, weakling little brother. But from the expressions on their faces it looked like they'd finally figured out she was female.

"Geez, Franny." Apparently Joe had managed to catch his breath and find his voice.

Tony looked incapable of saying anything.

Carlo was wearing that suspicious, interrogation face of his, eyes narrowed and one brow winging upward.

On her left, her brother Nicky took his cloth napkin and dropped it over her cleavage. The napkin held a moment then slid to her lap.

Francesca threw it back at him before daring to look at her father.

His expression unreadable, she tensed. Then she thought she saw his eyes water. He reached for the handkerchief in his back pocket and made a quick swipe across his face. Then he beamed.

"*Bella.* Beautiful. A beautiful woman just like your mama."

"A woman? Franny?" Tony hooted, obviously working up to an unmerciful tease.

Pop held up his hand. "You show your sister some respect." He sent all of her brothers a stern look. "Enough. Now eat."

Not until she heard the obedient scrape of forks against plates did Francesca slide a glance at Brett.

He hadn't picked up a single utensil. In fact, she doubted he'd moved since he'd dropped her apron on the floor beside her chair. She leaned over to retrieve it and found his hand there first. Their gazes met over the apron's striped denim.

"*Bella,*" he said softly.

Her mouth dried, and she licked her lips to wet them.

He followed the movement with his eyes. "*Bella* there, too."

For lack of a better response, Francesca smiled.

He smiled in return, then straightened.

To recover from the dazzling whiteness and the whispered word, Francesca gave herself another moment below table level. Then with a fortifying breath, she sat up and applied her attention to her plate.

Or tried to.

But from the corner of her eye she was continually distracted by Brett's tanned and capable hands. With her brothers, she never noticed how they held their knives, never noticed how often they took a sip of red wine, but she found herself fascinated by Brett's every move.

Gluing her gaze to her plate, she moved around lasagna and lettuce leaves, a giddiness in her stomach leaving no room for food. A gulp, then several more gulps of the full-bodied cabernet didn't seem to help. Warmth radiated out from her belly, and the wine gave her the guts to slide another look Brett's way.

He was staring at her.

The sounds at the table receded. Far in the background she heard the clatter of china. The bark of male laughter. A brother asking for more lasagna and another telling someone to pass the wine. It was the familiar music of her life and it faded to a mere buzz in comparison to the high-volume message coming out of Brett's eyes: *I like what I see.*

And though maybe she'd misinterpreted him, the exposed skin of her shoulders and chest tingled in response.

She knew the instant he noticed the chills. His knuckles turned white where he gripped his fork. His nostrils flared just the tiniest, the movement so sexual that Francesca's mouth went arid again and she blindly reached for her goblet to toss back the rest of her wine.

Licking a last drop from her bottom lip, she madly tried resurrecting her initial intention. *A brother, a brother, a brother!*

But how could a woman treat a man like a brother when he looked at her like she was a queen?

WHEN THE MEAL was finally over, Francesca found enough good sense to get away from the men by trading Tony, Joe and Nicky dish duty in return for a detailed cleaning of her truck the next afternoon. Back in the kitchen, with her voluminous apron rewrapped and wearing oversize yellow rubber gloves to protect her new manicure, Francesca regained her perspective and a fingernail hold on her control.

A dress didn't change anything. Gauche inside a gorgeous package was still just...gauche. And gauche couldn't sustain the interest of a man like Brett.

Any minute now he would take his leave or, if he settled in around Pop's TV like her brothers, then she could always slip back to her own apartment through the kitchen's back door. Away from Brett she'd feel more like herself.

She tried not to worry when Brett pushed through the

swinging kitchen door, bearing the last stack of plates in his hands.

Cautious, though, she kept her eyes on the water running into the kitchen sink. She pointed one yellow, floppy rubber fingertip in the direction of the counter. "Right there, please," she said cheerfully, fully expecting him to follow her direction and then make an immediate about-face to the living room.

Instead, he paused after depositing the dishes.

She felt him there, hovering, but she steadfastly refused to turn his way and continued sliding the rinsed plates into the small dishwasher.

Finally he spoke. "Where are the dish towels?"

Unable to stifle her amazement, Francesca spun around. "A man requesting dish towels? I should faint with shock!"

He grinned and sidled closer. "Goody. Then I'd have to catch you." His comic leer made her giggle.

And then it made her get nervous. "No, no, no," she protested. "You're the guest. No catching the cook or helping with the dishes."

He shook his head. "I'd deem it an honor."

Which one? Doing the dishes or putting his arms around her?

Francesca decided not to ask. And then she couldn't talk as he edged closer. She tried moving away, but the sink was at her back and the countertop pressed against her spine.

She held up her hands to warn him off, but in the big

yellow gloves they appeared clownlike instead of serious. With his thumb and forefinger he pinched one rubbery tip of each glove and drew them off her hands.

"You're done," he said.

Oh, she was. Done with the silly brother stuff. Done with thinking she could control her reaction to him. Done trying to stop her heart from pounding so darn hard that she couldn't hear anything but its beat in her ears.

She looked up into those blue, blue eyes of his. She saw her reflection there and thought, for the first time, she looked different. Really different. In Brett's eyes, Francesca saw herself as a woman, a woman with a sexy curve to her hair and a sensuous smile on her lips.

Her reflection boosted her confidence. Maybe this was what she looked like to him. Maybe this was who she was to him.

The idea gave her the courage to follow her desire.

As if he'd made her hands naked just for this, she slid both arms around his shoulders and touched her palms to the silky blond hair at the back of his head. She pulled him down for her kiss.

Maybe it didn't explode right away. She had to kind of slide her mouth over his hard cheek to locate his lips—but once she found his mouth the kiss ignited. She pressed against his lips harder. He pressed back.

He wasn't close enough to her. She tried dragging his solid body closer, but when that got her nowhere she moved forward to him. Her mouth opened against his, the woman she'd seen in his eyes giving him every bit of a woman's kiss. It was every bit a woman's instinct, too, that drove her to lean into him and entwine one leg around the back of his calf.

But then, just as the heat between them started to boil, it was very much a man's move—Carlo's move—that suddenly wrenched Brett away from her and planted a big brother's fist square against his jaw.

5

STUNNED, BRETT STOOD in Pop Milano's kitchen, breathing hard, and as much staggered by Francesca's kiss as he was by Carlo's fist. God, he might have laughed at the tableau the three of them made if his jaw wasn't throbbing like hell. Carlo, bellow-breathing like an enraged bull. Francesca, grown-up looking in her cut-to-there dress, but in wide-eyed innocence over what that dress—that *bella* dress—had wrought.

As for him—well, Brett guessed he was the villain of the piece.

Francesca moved first. *"Carlo!"* She planted her hands on her hips, and her dark eyes flashed fire in her brother's direction. "How *dare* you!"

He sputtered a bit, but what Carlo didn't dare was protest as Francesca grabbed Brett by the arm and dragged him out the kitchen's back door.

"Hey, hey!" Brett tried halting her momentum, but she sent him a quelling look and just tightened her grip on him. Well, he figured he owed her the first apology and so let her lead him in the direction of her apartment, the full skirt of her tropical print dress billowing behind her.

In seconds he was in her small kitchen beside a table the size of a TV dinner. She forced him to sit on a straight-backed chair with a no-nonsense shove against his shoulder. Before he could blink she—*splat!*—slapped a bag of frozen peas against his aching jaw.

"Oof!" He couldn't stifle an involuntary wince as he held the bag there.

All the starch went out of her. "Oh!" Her shoulders drooped and she dropped into the chair beside his. "I'm sorry. I'm so mad at Carlo that I was taking it out on you."

The frozen peas crunched against each other as he spoke. "Listen Francesca, I should be the one to apologize."

Her eyes widened in surprise. "No—"

"Yes. It's natural for your brothers to want to protect you." He didn't add that he felt the impulse in spades himself. "I shouldn't have put you in an, uh, uncomfortable position."

Color flagged her golden cheekbones. "Wait a minute—"

"I'm just saying that you shouldn't be mad at Carlo. And I hope you'll accept *my* apology for, well, *compromising* you in your father's kitchen."

"Hold it!" That fire had returned to her eyes and it looked hot enough to make instant green pea casserole. "Are you telling me that you're sorry for kissing me?"

"Well, uh, yeah."

She slapped her palms against the tabletop. "Well that

just about does it.'' Her full upper lip curled in disgust. ''I can't even get getting-caught right!''

Get getting-caught right? ''Francesca?''

She ignored him, instead rising from her chair to pace away from him. ''Other women are caught kissing when they're fourteen. It finally happens to me and you ruin it!''

He'd ruined it? Brett moved the frozen peas to his forehead thinking the cold might clear his confusion. Nope, no help. ''I ruined it, you said?''

She continued striding away from him. ''Of course you did!''

''Uh, Francesca?''

She reached the sink and spun around, breathing so hard he found he couldn't look away from the smooth skin of her cleavage, rising at dangerous levels over the top of her dress. She glowered at him. ''What?''

He tossed the peas on the table. ''When we were... 'caught,' exactly what did I do wrong?''

''The fist in the face aside—'' she crossed her arms over her chest, pushing up her breasts more fateful inches ''—I'd think you'd be embarrassed, still aroused maybe, but not apologetic!''

As if she could see he utterly lacked a clue, she frowned and blew out a long breath of frustrated air. ''Brett, for the first time in my entire life I was doing something womanly and a little bit...wild and you've taken the glory out of it!''

What did that make? Five or six hundred times she'd

poleaxed him today? The low-cut dress and every breath she took in the sexy thing, that whopper of a kiss, this whole "glory" business.

He shook his head. "Francesca, what am I going to do with you?"

She pursed her lips as if deciding how to respond. Then she said, "I kind of hoped we were doing it." Pink color flooded her face. "Before Carlo came in, I mean."

Well, hell. A woman dressed like an exotic, tropical temptation. The recent memory of the best-tasting kisses of his life.

He was a marshmallow when it came to Francesca.

She must have seen it on his face, because she crossed the kitchen floor in two speedy heartbeats. One forefinger trailed gently over his jaw. "Let me kiss it?"

He pulled her onto his lap.

Fragrant and small, she nestled easily against his chest and looped her arms around his neck. Then she smiled at him.

He cleared his throat. "So you think you can make it better?"

Her smile went from womanly to wicked. "I know I can," she said.

That's when he stopped thinking. His heart slammed against his chest, his lungs struggled for oxygen, and he pretty much figured he needed Francesca to save him.

Her mouth began the rescue mission.

As promised, she touched the injured part of his face first, but it wasn't the kind of twinge he expected when she flattened her tongue against his jawline. His thighs and groin tightened, and she rocked against his lap just as her lips found their way to his.

Like earlier in the kitchen, he let her control the kiss. Not because he wanted her to lead, but because he was afraid he might frighten her if *he* did. Her tongue experimented again, teasing the corners of his mouth, washing across his bottom lip.

He groaned when she tickled the seam between his lips, and he opened for her, but she ran away from a deeper kiss, moving her mouth to plant baby kisses up his other jawline in the direction of his ear.

She whispered to him, her breath sending waves of heat rolling across his skin. "Thank you, Brett," she said.

Thanks for the burning pleasure *she* gave *him?* His arms were circling her slender waist, and he didn't allow himself to explore her any further. "Francesca…"

"Shh." She placed two fingers over his mouth. "Don't say anything. Don't think anything. I need the experience."

He groaned again. Like a kitten flexing her claws, she wanted to see how deep she could dig. What kind of pleasure she could have.

She wanted experience, and she wanted it with him. If he didn't give in, who would she go to?

Don't think. The words echoed, and Brett couldn't resist drawing one of Francesca's fingers—still so conveniently placed against his lips—into his mouth.

She gasped. He saw her stiffen and then her eyes closed when he rubbed his tongue along the sensitive inner skin between her fingers. A flush brightened her cheeks, and he watched it deepen as he sucked, holding her small finger against the roof of his mouth with his tongue.

He took one of his arms from around her waist. He circled her wrist and drew her finger from his mouth. Her eyes opened, and he watched them closely as he directed her wet fingertip to her own skin, letting it paint a damp line on her fragile collarbone.

Her pupils dilated, and chills chased one another down her neck and into the low-cut bodice of her dress.

Brett could hear his own harsh breathing and he stilled, making an effort to slow down.

''Brett?'' she whispered. Not a shred of doubt colored her voice, only the sweet demand of desire.

He smoothed his palm over her hair. ''Francesca.''

She frowned a little bit. ''Kiss me some more, Brett.''

He smiled. ''I haven't kissed you at all.''

Her frown deepened. ''Well, whatever you call it, I want some more.''

God, she made him laugh. ''That sounds like an order.''

''It is.''

He laughed again. His tomboy princess. ''Your wish is my command,'' he said, and then he brushed back the hair from her face and kissed her nose, her cheeks and then finally explored the dainty curl of one ear.

Her nails dug into his upper arms as he nipped on her earlobe, and the little pain mirrored the good ache in his groin. Beneath her hips he shifted a little in the chair, and she wiggled, too, until his arousal settled into the warm notch of her thighs.

He groaned.

Her eyelashes flew open. "Am I too heavy?"

He didn't want her going anywhere, so he ran a fingertip down the slope of her shoulder as distraction. "Not a chance," he said, and then his finger met the skinny strap of her dress and the strap slid off her shoulder.

They both froze.

Then Brett lifted his other hand to surf the line of her opposite shoulder. He flicked the strap there and it dropped down, too. Above the bodice of her dress the roundness of Francesca's breasts rose and fell with even quicker breaths.

"Kiss me, Brett," she demanded.

With a hand cupping each bare shoulder he did, and her mouth softened immediately, opening for him. He thrust inside, turned on so damn bad now with her bare skin against his palms, with her fragrance rising around him like a soft cloud of arousal.

She moaned when he lifted his mouth, and then again when he slid kiss after kiss against the skin of her neck.

Her hands moved across his back and she pulled impatiently at his shirt. But she tasted too good to abandon, so he kept kissing her neck and shoulders until she pulled his knit shirt free from his jeans and pushed it upward.

Her palms burned him wherever she touched—so, so good—and he pulled away just for the instant it took to throw off his shirt. Now she found his mouth and her hands explored his chest, teasing him with a light, wondering touch.

His blood burned, his groin tightened rock hard, and as she ran her little hands up his skin, his fingers found the back zipper of her dress. The rasp as he drew it down didn't register over the syncopated hoarseness of their breaths.

He curled his fingers into the neckline then thrust his tongue into Francesca's mouth just as he jerked the dress to her waist. With one more quick movement the naked, hot skin of her breasts met his chest.

"Brett."

He barely heard the sweet exclamation over the exhilarated scream of every nerve ending in his body. Francesca's breasts were round and swollen, and the hard nubs of her nipples pressed into him like the very best kind of torture.

He twisted his torso so they grazed each other's skin.

"Brett."

Francesca's eyes were secret-dark, the pupils dilated with desire. He pulled back, eager to hold the fullness of her breasts in his hand, to taste the hard nipples. She watched him, her face completely trusting.

So trusting.

Damn, damn, *damn* trusting.

Wasn't this the very thing he was supposed to be protecting her from?

Closing his eyes and gritting his teeth, Brett made himself draw up her bodice. Made himself zip the damned enticing dress. Made himself lift her off his lap with only one more sweet, gentle kiss to her lips.

Made himself promise he'd never touch her like that again.

FRANCESCA FOUND herself thrust into the chair beside Brett's, still gasping for breath, her skin still tingling from his touch. Her dress was rezipped too, so she just blinked dizzily at him as he felt around for his shirt on the floor beneath him. He pulled it on, and a little sigh escaped her.

She thought he heard the sound, but he didn't look at her. Instead, he scrubbed his face with his hands and raked his fingers through his dark blond hair.

It had felt smooth and springy between her fingers. She sighed again.

His blue eyes cut her way. "Francesca…" He scrubbed his face again and inhaled a deep breath.

She watched his chest slowly rise and fall. It had been hard and hot beneath her hands and like…nothing she could describe when he'd rubbed it against her breasts. She allowed herself just one more sigh.

He groaned. "*Francesca.* You're not making this easy for me."

Well, good. It wasn't easy for her to come down from a desire high, either. Especially when it wasn't her idea.

Brett took another deep breath. "Okay. I'm going to say this and then get out of here. Francesca, I am very, very sor—"

"No!" She threw him a murderous look. "Don't you *dare* say that word."

"Francesca—"

"Don't." She shook her head for emphasis. "Or I'll put my fingers in my ears and hum 'The Star Spangled Banner.'" If he tried apologizing again her ego would shrivel to the size of a raisin. She didn't need that right now, not when she was still reeling from a passion she didn't even realize she had inside her.

She jumped up from her seat. "Let me make us some coffee instead."

Now *he* sighed. "If you're not going to let me talk, I should really be leaving."

"Talk? Who said we couldn't talk?"

He narrowed his eyes. "You're not going to hum or anything?"

She made her most serious face. "No humming, I promise. But I always reserve the right to break into song."

He laughed, and for the first time since they'd stopped kissing she saw him relax.

Good. She crossed to her small pantry to search for the coffee filters. The last thing she wanted—after an apology, that is—was for him to be tense around her.

Not when *she* really *did* want to sing and then shriek and then Snoopy-dance with joy.

Brett had kissed her and touched her and gone up in the same flames she had.

A woman who had doubted her ability to attract men—a woman who had dreamed about attracting *this* man since she was twelve years old—could only be ecstatic about that.

Scooping coffee grounds with a hand that still tremored, Francesca acknowledged that Brett might not be as thrilled as she. Most likely the last woman in his arms had been the beautiful love of his life, Patricia.

Certainly Francesca couldn't compare to her.

But if she let him back away right now she might never get another chance with him. It didn't take years of experience to realize that the moment he began seeing her as a woman was no time to let him get away.

So, MOMENTS LATER, with two oversize blue-and-yellow ceramic cups between them, Francesca smiled at Brett brightly. ''There,'' she said. She took a sip of her milk-laced coffee, peeking at him over the brim. Time to talk. Get to know each other as adults. Work, books, movies. She'd even be willing to discuss sports teams if she had to.

He wrapped his palms around his cup. ''About what just happened…''

Francesca almost choked on her coffee. As it was, she

had to swallow quickly and set the cup down with a clatter onto the matching saucer. "What?"

"We need to talk about it, Francesca."

"Oh, please." Her face warmed. "Could we do without the recriminations?"

Something passed over his face that looked like pain. "I don't know."

"Look, Brett. It happened, okay? It was good..."

His gorgeous mouth moved in a rueful grin. "So now let's forget about it?"

That wasn't exactly what she had in mind. Next he'd say they should make sure it never happened again.

He leaned forward. "Listen. I'm at a different place in my life, and—" He hesitated.

Terrific. Here came the "it should never happen again" part. Probably followed by a whole bunch of stuff about the wonderful Patricia. Francesca's heart twisted. She just couldn't bear hearing it right now.

She hopped up. "Speaking of different places in life. Wait'll you see what I have."

Bless him for indulging her avoidance. She scurried to the living room bookshelf and retrieved a photo album. She'd made one for each brother and then herself last Christmas, after finally going through the shoeboxes full of family pictures that no one had bothered sorting in over twenty years.

She laid the album on the table in front of Brett. "I think you show up more in the boys' albums, but I just *know* there are some photos of you in here."

Leaning against the wall behind him, she let Brett turn the pages. As the youngest of five children, there were few baby pictures of her. "Pop said we all looked the same when we wore only diapers and dimples," she told Brett, but he still got a chuckle over the one bare-behind-on-the-bearskin shot.

But his laughter quieted when he came across a photograph of Francesca's mother, Dina. Silently he traced the edges of the picture with one forefinger. Then he cleared his throat. "I remember her. Your mom."

From her position she could only see the side of Brett's face, but his cheek creased with a small smile. "She baked great chocolate chip cookies and made the best spaghetti I've ever tasted. And..." He stopped.

Francesca tried swallowing away the sticky lump in her throat. Her brothers and Pop rarely talked about their mom in front of her and she suspected it was because they didn't want her to know what she'd missed. "And?" she prompted. "Spaghetti and cookies and what else?"

"And your father was right. She was beautiful. Just like you."

Lucky she was leaning against the wall, or else she'd be a messy puddle at Brett's feet. She swallowed again. "Thank you," she whispered.

He acted as if he didn't hear her, going ahead to turn the pages of their childhood. He was present in a lot of the group shots: around the Milano Christmas tree, beside the grinning jack-o'-lanterns, in a baseball uniform on one of the many teams Pop had coached.

He pointed to one particularly unflattering shot of Francesca. "You haven't changed much."

She groaned. "Oh, yeah, that's me all right. With a Band-Aid on each knee and a prematurely missing tooth."

"Joe knocked it out with an elbow."

"How'd you remember?"

Brett shook his head. "Because I never heard anyone scream so loud in my life. Scared me to death. Your brothers scoured the grass for the tooth but I couldn't move."

She remembered as if it was yesterday. She'd been about five years old, and while everybody else was looking for the tooth, Brett had mopped up the blood and her tears. "You held my hand all afternoon," she said.

"And the other one I clapped over my ears." He gave her a self-deprecating grin.

He didn't want her to see him as a hero. But he'd been that for her when she was growing up. And somewhere between four and twelve she'd gone from hero worship to puppy love.

And somewhere in the past few days she'd gone to—

"Hey! This looks familiar."

Francesca peered over his shoulder. "Oh, yuck," she said. "My sixth-grade school picture." Braces, goofy hair in what some backward beautician had called a "pixie" cut. Francesca also sported a caged expression and one of Carlo's too-big shirts. "Poor Pop. He always tried to get me into dresses for picture day but I was slippier than an eel."

"Wait a minute," Brett said, lifting one hip off his chair to slide his billfold from his back pocket. "Guess what I have."

He shuffled through a wad of the stuff that gathered in wallets: receipts, credit and business cards. "Hah!" he finally exclaimed, and tossed something to the table-top.

That exact same sixth-grade photo of her. Except this one had a "Love, Francesca" written across the bottom and "To My Main Squeeze, Brett," across the top. The *i* in *main* was dotted with a heart.

He sent her a triumphant look. "That was my going-away-to-college present."

Francesca sat down in the chair beside Brett's, half embarrassed, half pleased that he'd kept it all these years. "My sincere apologies."

He frowned slightly as he tried to shove the remainder of the stuff back into his wallet. "I thought we weren't going to apolog—"

The stack got away from him and scattered over the table. Gas cards. ATM receipts. A studio shot of Brett's golden-haired Patricia landed inches from the photo capturing Francesca's preteen pain.

Her heart stopped beating.

"I thought I'd taken this out," he said quickly, reaching for Patricia's picture.

Francesca beat him to it. She cradled the photo in her hand, her heart restarting sluggishly as she registered the woman's smooth blond hair, toothpaste smile, the lace collar of her dress and perfectly manicured nails. "She was lovely."

"Yes," Brett said quietly.

Francesca gulped. "She was everything I always wanted to be, but didn't know how."

"I didn't even know you knew her."

Francesca shook her head. "I didn't, not really. But your senior year I went to the homecoming game with Pop and the brothers. I was just at the right age to be dazzled by the Homecoming Queen."

"Ah. But I would never have taken you for a Homecoming Queen wanna-be."

She didn't look at him. "Now that's where you're wrong. There's nothing I ever wanted to be more than a queen. Or a princess, even."

"You were the queen of the Milano household, that's for sure."

She threw him a disgusted look. "No. I wanted to be *real* royalty. Well, high school royalty. I wanted a crown and a corsage and at least once I wanted to ride in a limo with…"

"A prince?"

That would do. "Right." Not any old prince, though. She'd wanted Prince Brett.

''Francesca,'' he breathed her name softly, as if he didn't know what else to say.

She met his eyes. ''Pretty silly, huh?''

He shrugged. ''Just surprising.''

She shrugged too. ''Well, it was so surprising that not a bit of it ever happened. No crowns, no limos, not even one measly date to the prom.'' She slid Patricia's picture back toward Brett.

Instead of reinserting it into his wallet, he absentmindedly shoved it in his back pocket. ''I don't believe you didn't go to the prom.''

''Nobody asked me. To help them tune up their car, yes. But to a dance? To a place I'd be required to wear a dress?'' She shook her head. ''I don't think it ever occurred to any boy I knew.''

He smiled, reaching out to lightly touch her tropical print skirt. ''Their loss.''

She ducked their head. ''I'm more suited to jeans,'' she mumbled.

There was a moment of silence, then Brett spoke. ''Maybe,'' he said, chucking her under the chin. ''But I like you just the way you are.''

After a stunned moment, Francesca's temper ignited. He'd actually *chucked her under the chin!* She looked up, staring at the now-avuncular and slightly superior expression on his face. If she'd been twelve she would have landed him a facer to match Carlo's for the stupid gesture.

And then she absorbed what he'd said. *I like you just the way you are.*

Her temper flared higher. She wanted to scream. She wanted to cry. Punching sounded awfully good again.

Because ''liking'' wasn't the feeling she wanted from Brett, particularly not in that placating, almost-condescending way. Yes, as a testament from the man who had just an hour ago brought you closer to ecstasy than at any moment in your entire life, it was a mouthful of mere ashes.

6

BRETT TURNED into the apartment parking lot, burned out and ticked off after three fourteen-hour days on a case that had blown up in their faces when a witness recanted his testimony. He was not in a good mood and it turned even lousier when the first mug he should see once he exited his car was the one owned by the guy who had given him a face plant four days before.

Carlo.

Brett let out a sigh, then dropped his briefcase to the pavement. "If this is round two, let me just say that I've had a bad day and I'd be honored to take it out on your nose."

Carlo stepped into the circle of the security light illuminating the 10:00 p.m. darkness and shoved one big hand into the front pocket of his jeans. "Naw. I'm here to apologize." He rubbed the back of his neck with his free hand. "I've been a little edgy lately."

Brett bent to retrieve his briefcase. "Well, if we're offering up apologies, I guess I should—"

"Don't." Carlo shook his head. "Franny read me the riot act. She said the uh, situation was all her fault *and* made me promise not to let you apologize, either. She was adamant about that.''

That sounded like Francesca. The adamant-about-apologies part. But the kiss being all her fault? Well, maybe that one had been, but God knew that Brett was responsible for all the rest. All the rest that had severely impacted his ability to sleep the last few nights.

But he would stay away from her. What had started out as a white-knight impulse had escalated into a white-hot lust that he had no business feeling for Francesca. She deserved candy and flowers and forever, and he was incapable of promising that.

Brett looked over at Carlo. ''You up for a beer?'' This was the Milano he could afford to spend time with. From now on, Francesca was off-limits.

Carlo relaxed, as if the weight of the world was lifted from his shoulders. ''You just caught me leaving. I'm meeting Joe and Tony at the tavern for some beers and pool. Wanna come?''

Brett opened his mouth to answer. But then a car zoomed—too fast—into the parking lot and halted with a squeal of brakes. From a couple of cars away, Brett could see Francesca in the passenger seat, laughing at something the hot-rodder said.

Brett felt the beginnings of a burn in his gut. ''Who's that?'' he asked Carlo.

''Franny.''

Brett rolled his eyes in the other man's direction. ''I mean, *who* is that with her?''

Carlo shrugged. ''I don't know. You coming with me, or what?''

Francesca was still laughing. She reached over the back of the seat and pulled something into her arms—it looked like clothes. Then she disappeared down into her seat. He couldn't even form in his head what she might be doing now, but that beginning of an ulcer started gnawing at his belly again.

Annoyed, he stared at Carlo. ''It's okay for her to be with some stranger, but you throw a punch at *me?*''

''There's no kissing involved.''

Well, B.S. Because as Brett watched she leaned over and bussed the guy on the cheek before jumping out of the car. Then, with her finger hooked over the hanger of some plastic-encased garment, she leaned into the car. Her cute little tush piked into the air, she chattered at the guy a mile a minute, probably charming him, making him smile, making him laugh, making him willing to do anything to win her that bet she'd made with Carlo.

That bet.

He nearly groaned out loud. There was still the problem of that bet. With Brett bowing out of her life, she'd be looking to fill the void and find a man.

''Brett?'' Carlo sent him a puzzled look, as if he'd been calling his name several times.

With a final cheerful wave of her hand, Francesca dismissed her Daytona driver wanna-be. She disappeared in the direction of her apartment without even acknowledging her brother or Brett.

''Brett?'' Carlo again. ''Are you coming out for a drink or not?''

''Not,'' he said absently, following in Francesca's wake.

FRANCESCA FUMBLED with her keys. Darn Brett. Just catching a glimpse of him after four days could set her hands trembling. From where he had been standing in the parking lot with Carlo, she couldn't tell whether he was coming or going, but she wasn't taking any chances.

Get in the apartment in case he happened by!

She didn't want to see him. He'd shown up with plenty of regularity in her dreams the past few nights, and she was hoping that time apart from him would bring about The Cure.

The Cure. That's what Elise claimed Francesca needed. Not that she'd gone into great detail about what had happened between Brett and her, but just a few choice words and Elise had seemed to grasp the picture. And The Cure had been her solution.

Ah. The key finally fit in the lock just as she glimpsed Brett coming in her direction. She slipped inside the door and slammed it shut behind her. Nothing could have stopped her from peering out the peephole, though. And yep, there he was.

Blue-eyed, Scandinavian-beautiful Brett, all clean cheekbones and broad shoulders. Her heart started skipping around again and she forced herself away and toward the kitchen. Toward The Cure.

She carefully hung her third and thankfully last bridesmaid's dress from the top of the pantry door. She'd have started The Cure this moment, but Elise swore it required a full evening, and Francesca was worn out after a final fitting of the dress and a night out with the other women of the wedding party.

Rubbing her palms against her jeans, she turned to contemplate the kitchen table and The Cure ingredients. The phone rang and Francesca absently picked it up.

"Who was that?" said the caller.

"Brett?" The sound of his voice sent a betraying set of chills down her spine. Francesca frowned at the phone. "How'd you get my number?"

"You're in the phone book."

"Oh." Sheesh, of course. Hearing his voice again made her silly. "That's right."

"No, that's wrong." Brett didn't sound like he had a good hold on his patience. "It's not even listed as 'F. Milano.' It says plain, old 'Francesca.'"

"That's me. Plain old Francesca."

He made a noise suspiciously like a snort.

"I gotta go, Brett." Francesca swung back in the direction of her Cure ingredients. When you needed to get a man off your mind, Elise had the answer. First you had to get him out of your sight and then you had to take The Cure. Francesca was pretty sure phone calls from said man were not part of the prescription.

"Just answer my question first."

From the table she retrieved Elise's handwritten list.

It had taken Francesca three stops and thirty dollars to fulfill the requirements, but if it worked, it was more than worth the cost.

"Who was that man?" Brett asked again, his voice surly.

Herbal face mask, check. Peach-pit exfoliating body cream, check. "What man?"

"The one who drove you home."

Hot-avocado oil hair treatment, this banana-scented stuff you put on the cuticles of your fingers and toes.

Francesca figured she knew how this Cure thing worked. It got men out of your life, all right. By turning you into a woman only a fruit-bat would love.

"You're not talking to me, Francesca."

Because I'm trying to forget about you. "A friend. He was a friend." From under the table she retrieved a little tube of cherry salve that was supposed to take years off your lips.

She'd settle for the removal of the memory of a few kisses.

"What are you doing tomorrow night?" Brett asked.

Francesca's shoulders slumped, and she collapsed into the chair beside the table. Not this again. "I'm busy," she said.

"With what?"

"I have plans." *Plans to take The Cure and rid you from my heart—no not heart—mind.*

"Plans with your 'friend'?"

Francesca felt her temper kindle. "To what purpose is this phone call?"

Now it was his turn to not answer.

"Are you checking up on me out of brotherly concern?" she said, exasperated. "Because if you are, I have more than my share of that overrated stuff."

Through the phone she heard him swallow. "I feel... differently from a brother."

Francesca's heart dropped to her stomach. She took a deep breath, hoping to lift it back into position. "Wh—" It took a moment to catch her breath. "What do you mean?"

"Hell, Francesca, I had you half-naked in my arms the other night. Surely you've got to know that wasn't *brotherly*."

Francesca flung out a hand and knocked over the bottle of face mask. "Of course, of course." She squeezed shut her eyes, not wanting to remember how easily he brought the passion out in her.

He groaned softly, as if he was picturing the same thing. "It just seems...dangerous, Francesca."

Her mouth was dry. "Dangerous, how?"

"You—" He broke off.

"What?"

"It's so hot, so fast." He cleared his throat. "Just forget I said that."

She wouldn't forget it as long as she lived. Because it told her something. It told her that Mr. Scandinavian

Blue-Eyed Calm wasn't as in control as he'd seemed the other night.

Francesca's heart had flown back up to its rightful place and now was flapping around in her chest like a butterfly gone suddenly free. She gripped the edge of the table. "Why don't you come over, Brett?"

"What?"

"Right now. Come over and be with me." She wanted to see him. She knew, just *knew* he wanted to see her.

Silence stretched out across the line.

"Please," she cajoled, not caring a whit about her pride or any female don't-ask-first games that she'd heard her friends advise each other about all her life.

She'd been raised by men. "What do you say, Brett?" Straightforward, direct men, who'd taught her that those who don't ask, don't get. Even so, she held her breath, willing him to agree.

"I say no."

"No?" Embarrassment burned hot patches on her cheeks and the back of her neck. "You're rejecting me?" she whispered.

"No! *Not* rejecting you, Francesca, but—"

He was still talking as she hung up.

The phone rang again. She didn't answer. It rang some more. She wouldn't answer.

She was too busy lining up the bottles and potions of The Cure. Elise had promised it would work. Francesca wasn't so sure.

Maybe it was her Italian blood, but Francesca thought the whole process needed something.

She got out a cookbook. Her mother had baked chocolate chip cookies. And Francesca made cannolli that everybody swore kicked butt.

IN THE MORNING Elise brought over brownies. With the psychic connection that signified a true best friend, Elise just showed up at Francesca's door with a plate of the fudgy walnut squares *her* mother was famous for.

"She's sabotaging me!" Elise shrieked. Apparently their psychic link was on the blink because Francesca hadn't a clue what Elise was talking about, and Elise didn't seem to realize that Francesca was deep in the dumps herself.

Francesca led the way to the kitchen and automatically filled the teakettle. "Who and why?" she asked.

"The woman who made these tempting things, that's who! My mother who is paying for a wedding dress that isn't going to fit me after I down these brownies!"

Francesca patted her best friend on the shoulder and took the brownies away from her. "Don't eat them."

"Bridal jitters are worse than a bad case of PMS!" Elise said, grabbing back the plate. "I need this food."

"You don't," she said, pulling the plate away.

Elise wrestled the brownies back again. "Franny, you *know* sometimes we just gotta have the worst thing for us."

Francesca opened her mouth to respond, but her door-bell rang.

Afraid to leave Elise alone too long, Francesca ran to answer it. On her doorstep stood a delivery girl holding a vase containing a huge spray of pink wildflowers sur-rounding one perfect pink rose. Francesca blinked. "These can't be for me."

Elise came up behind her. "Of course they can, you ninny. Your name is on the delivery sheet. Now sign for them."

Stunned, Francesca obeyed, then shut the door and carried the flowers into the kitchen. The kettle was whis-tling, so she set the flowers down on the table and began to make tea.

Elise stared at her. "What are you doing? Don't you want to open the card?"

The card. Of course. Flowers came with a card and you opened it and it told you who they were from. It was just that she'd had little experience receiving flow-ers.

No experience, to be precise.

She wiped her hands on a dish towel and found the tiny card, perched on a plastic fork thing nestled amidst the arrangement. The tiny wildflowers trembled on their stalks as she tried to gently work the card free.

"Oh, come on!" Elise snatched the card out of the flowers and handed it over to Francesca. "Let's see what it says."

The little envelope was sealed. Even though she'd

given up biting her nails, Francesca couldn't get enough of a grip to open the flap. She bit her lip, looking for the best place to begin.

"Oh, my God!" Apparently those jitters really had hold of Elise. She took the envelope from Francesca and instantly ripped it open and pulled out the card. "Here."

"Sorry," it said. "Forgive me?" in a masculine slash.

Brett wanted her to forgive him. Before Francesca could decide if she did or not, the front bell rang again.

"I'll get it." Elise ran to the door and in seconds was back. "Another florist," she said. She thrust a small cool box into Francesca's hands.

Francesca slipped into a chair and set the white box on the tabletop. Conscious of the impatient Elise, she worked quicker now and opened the lid to find the most beautiful creation inside. More pink roses, one in full bloom and two half-opened blossoms, cunningly set with delicate bows of tulle ribbon and a circle of silver elastic.

"It's a wrist corsage," Elise said. "Who is sending you a wrist corsage? And *why* is someone sending you one?"

A corsage. Francesca touched the edge of the fragile ribbon. She'd never had one before. She'd always wanted one. She'd told Brett.

"Look." Elise pointed to another tiny card tucked into the box.

No envelope this time. "Be my date tonight?"

Francesca's heart clenched. The doorbell rang again.

"This is getting good." Elise ran for the door and

was back in seconds. "No flowers this time. Just some generic delivery guy."

Another box, this one larger and wrapped in silver paper with a big pink bow. Francesca's palms started to sweat. She pushed it toward Elise. "You open it."

"No way. Just hurry up."

Francesca took a breath and tore into the paper. Then opened the lid of the box. And almost suffocated by forgetting to take a second breath.

The box was filled with silver-spangled tissue paper. And cushioned in the middle of it was a rhinestone tiara. The most sparkly, delicate and fantasy-fulfilling crown that Francesca had ever seen.

Even Elise was speechless.

Inside this box was a card too. "Be my princess tonight."

Both Elise and Francesca reached for a brownie at the same instant. Their eyes met as they both took huge, chocolaty bites.

"This is from Brett," Elise said around her mouthful.

Francesca nodded.

"Brett whom you're supposed to be taking The Cure from tonight."

Francesca nodded again.

Elise looked back at what had just been delivered. Francesca followed her gaze. Flowers, corsage, crown. They sighed together.

"Well?" Elise said, the question in her eyes.

Francesca held up her brownie. "You said it, Elise. Sometimes we just gotta have the worst thing for us."

BRETT KNOCKED on the Plexiglas shield to signal the limo driver to stop in the apartment parking lot. Then Brett exited the long white car.

He couldn't let Francesca feel he'd rejected her. God knew he'd caught her at a vulnerable time in her life, what with that stupid bet. He couldn't let himself pierce her heart when he was the one trying to protect it.

So he had to let her see that she attracted him. As dangerous as it could be, it seemed the right thing was to let her know he thought she was beautiful and desirable.

Tonight the plan was to give her everything she'd yearned for. The corsage, the crown, the ride in the limo. It didn't take a great intellect to see Francesca thought those were the things that would make her a woman.

Those and a man's desire.

That was the easy part. Tonight Brett would let her see what she did to him. He wouldn't go too far, but just far enough for her to know what power she had. And then he'd let her go.

He walked toward Francesca's apartment, promising himself to get this evening right. At midnight the princess would realize she really *was* one, and then she could move on to find her future prince.

FRANCESCA FIDGETED, impatient for Brett to pick her up. She inspected the contents of her purse, adjusted the strap of her new sandals, found a tissue to wipe the persistent dampness from her palms. Finally she returned to her bedroom to admire the sparkle of the tiara Brett had sent. It sat upon her pillow, winking at her in the fading light, as if it knew something that she didn't.

She wanted to get on with the date. Not that she had any idea why she was so anxious for it to begin. Without a clue as to how she wanted to behave toward Brett, or of what she expected or wanted from him, it might be better if their evening out was postponed until she had a plan.

Still, she paced quickly back to the living room. At the front door she went on tiptoe and put one eye to the peephole. No Brett, not yet. Unable to contain her anxiousness, she opened her front door and peeked down the walkway.

He was heading her way.

Francesca whipped back inside and slammed the front door, squeezing shut her eyes.

It didn't help. *God.* She could still see him, his image burned upon her retinas. Brett, wearing a black tuxedo that lightened the burnished gold of his hair and made his eyes the blue of the kind of wicked promises a good girl wasn't supposed to want.

And suddenly, in the wink of a rhinestone, Francesca didn't want to be a good girl anymore.

Her heart started thrumming against her breastbone.

To put a finer point on it, she wanted to be bad with Brett.

She gulped, stunned by the instant, unwavering certitude. Maybe it wasn't the best idea that she'd ever had. Maybe not the most logical goal. But the second she'd seen him in that tuxedo, she'd immediately leaped to the idea of lying naked in his arms, and there came a sense, a rightness that she'd never experienced before.

Call it woman's intuition.

And she'd wanted to feel womanly her entire life.

Her hands started to tremble.

Brett. Her first lover was going to be Brett. It *had* to be Brett.

She racked her brain for every hint, any scrap of advice she'd ever heard or read. How did she make this happen? How could she make this evening end the way she wanted?

She took one last look in the mirror beside the door, too late rethinking the sweet pink of her dress, the long time she'd spent treading the safe and narrow.

Could Brett be persuaded to walk her over to the wild side?

And did she have the nerve to try?

BRETT BUTTONED the jacket of his tuxedo, then knocked on Francesca's door. His lips curved as the door swung inward, then the smile dropped away as his jaw fell open.

Damn.

He'd never seen a sight more gorgeous. A woman more arousing.

In a dress of transparent pink layers, Francesca looked like a fairy. Somewhere beneath the filmy stuff was a tight-fitting sheath that accentuated her sculpted body and revealed inches of that cleavage that constantly surprised him.

Her hair was swept up in a dark knot, and one wavy tendril floated over her cheek and pointed in the direction of her pink, wet-looking mouth.

Damn. He thought he was going to die.

Clearing his throat, he tried to get a hold of himself. ''Fr—'' The sound came out hoarse. ''Francesca,'' he finally said, clenching his fists to keep from reaching for her.

''Brett,'' she said softly, her little smile torture to him.

He tightened his fists again. Then suddenly it hit him. He didn't need to hold back. Tonight was all about *showing* her how she made him feel.

How she could make *any* man feel, he reminded himself.

He reached for her hand. It was warm and soft and the corsage on her wrist made her fingertips smell like roses. He flattened her palm against his cheek. ''I don't believe it.''

''Believe what?''

That she'd grown up. That she was here with him. That he could make it through tonight without going too far.

That he could *ever* let her go.

He shook his head to shake loose the thought. "The limo is waiting."

Her eyes widened. "No!"

He laughed. God, she enchanted him. "Of course. You said you wanted to ride in one."

She shut the door behind her, then stopped and looked at him suspiciously. "You're not taking me to a senior prom, are you? Because if you are I'll have to go back in and get my crown."

He laughed again. "No. That was just a...symbol. I thought we'd go to dinner and go dancing. Maybe ride around in the limo later."

She sighed dramatically. "A limo." She went on tip-toe to kiss his cheek. "Perfect."

That brief kiss zipped right into his bloodstream like a shot of whisky. He closed his eyes. If looking at her made him breathless, if her lips on his cheek made his blood heat, how would he survive the rest of the evening?

7

BRETT SURVIVED the evening with surprising ease, he discovered. Mostly because, unlike him, Francesca seemed completely unaffected by anything between them, fascinated instead by the limousine's accoutrements and the limousine driver himself.

She flipped through every TV channel, played several FM stations, inspected the crystal stemware, the appetizers, and refused a glass of chilled champagne. After the five minutes that took, she slid back the partition separating them from the driver and for the rest of the way to the restaurant quizzed the older man on how long he'd driven, whom he'd driven, and if he'd ever gotten lost.

Brett tried not to feel neglected. After all, this evening was about her. And she seemed to be having a good time, though slightly nervous. Through dinner she chattered away, entertaining him with wacky stories about apartment managing and the escapades of their mostly elderly tenants.

The limousine must have been a big hit for her, because after they ate she wanted to ride around in it instead of finding a dance club.

Bemused, Brett agreed. So much for the problems

he'd anticipated. Though he'd planned to show her his desire for her, he'd also worried that he might take it too far. As it was, she was treating him like one of the brothers she usually complained about.

She avoided his touch, avoided any kind of personal conversation. Back in the limo, she retreated to the farthest, darkest corner of the long seat. It was left to Brett to dim the interior lights and securely draw down the partition that gave them complete privacy.

Without asking, he poured her a glass of champagne. The limo smoothly rolled forward as he slid down her seat to hold it out to her.

Just as she leaned forward to reach for it, the limo took a quick corner, lurching her toward him.

There wasn't time for either one of them.

No time for her to catch herself.

No time for him to stop the champagne glass from falling to the carpeted floor.

No time for her to prevent herself from falling across him and no time for him to stop the instant hot reaction he had to Francesca lying across his lap.

He stared down at her dark and mysterious eyes. He watched her breasts rise and fall in a quick, involuntary breath.

And as if a switch had suddenly turned on, a high-voltage, sexual buzz filled the interior of the limo.

NERVOUS AS A DUCK in a pillow factory, all night long Francesca had babbled and forked food in her mouth and more than expressed her interest in the limousine, all because she didn't know how to let Brett know she wanted him.

That she meant to have him.

Thank goodness for that quick right turn. After a speedy mental promise to slip the limo driver a hefty tip, Francesca sank into the dizzying warmth of Brett's arms.

Heart accelerating, she tried to smile. "Well, hello."

There was blue fire in his eyes. "So you noticed I'm here."

Just every breath. Just every eyelash flutter and every movement of his long, strong fingers. "Yes," she said simply, still unsure how to proceed.

He pulled her closer against his chest. "Comfortable?" he asked.

She swallowed. *No.* She was edgy and nervous and she felt like she needed to shed her skin.

One of his forefingers traced the arch of her eyebrow. Heat shot from that single point of contact to radiate down her body.

"You're beautiful," he said, and there was something new and dark and exciting in his voice. "I want to kiss you."

"Oh?" she said quickly, her voice squeaking with nerves. *Oh?* She wanted to slap herself silly. What kind of response was "Oh?"

"What do you say?"

Say yes. Say please. Say take me. But her mouth

seemed to have a mind of its own. "I've never made out in a car," she said instead, all squeaky with anxiety again.

"No?" One of his eyebrows shot up, and he seemed calm, cool, collected, even amused. "It's highly overrated."

"Coming from one who knows?"

He grinned. "I've been a teenager, remember?"

She made a face. "Don't forget I was one, too."

His smile faded and he lifted her closer to him. "Francesca, I wish…"

Her heart kicked into the next higher gear. "You wish?"

But he didn't answer. "What happened?" he said instead. "That tuneups and dresses problem again? Why *didn't* you ever make out in a car?"

At her shrug, his grip tightened on her shoulders. He pulled her up so she sat in his lap instead of across his legs. "I hate myself for this," he said, frowning. "But I'm glad you haven't."

The protective comment didn't rankle. For the first time she didn't feel she'd missed out, not when she hoped Brett might rectify the situation any instant.

"Brett?"

He was staring into her face. "Mmm?"

"Didn't you say you wanted to kiss me?"

He groaned. "Francesca…"

Her heart slowed down a bit. "I don't like the sound of that."

"Isn't knowing I want to enough?"

No. Only all of him would be enough.

"Francesca, don't look at me like that...." He groaned again, as if he was in real pain.

Francesca's heart skidded to a halt. She licked her lips. "Is this—is this about Patricia?" she asked hesitantly. Great. Here she'd been only thinking of herself. Was it painful for Brett to be in another woman's arms?

He shook his head. "This is about *you*, Francesca. I promise. Only about *you*."

"Okay, then." In relief, she bounced a little against his lap.

"Francesca." Another long groan.

Uncertain, she froze, but then she thought about what she was feeling beneath her backside. Not just hard male thighs, but...hard male.

Maybe they weren't so far from the wild side after all.

She swallowed, steeling herself to be as direct as she had to be. As she wanted to be. "Brett," she said softly. "Thank you. Thank you for tonight. You fulfilled my teenage fantasies."

He pulled back his head, as if he realized something more was coming. "And? But? Though? However?" he said, looking at her suspiciously.

Francesca drew in a breath. A little do-or-die impulse had been nurtured in her from the day she opened her eyes and met the gazes of her four older brothers. It roared to life now, breathing enough dragon fire to cinderize any princessy qualms.

Just tell him what you want, the impulse prodded. *Ask for it.* You might not always win, taking on a challenge, but where was the glory in playing it safe?

She wet her lips again and tried looking assured. Whenever you went, um, guts to the wall, you had to be confident. She ran one fingertip across his cheekbone and watched the muscle in his jaw tick in reaction. You could be devious, too, if you needed to.

She smoothed back his hair. "Come on, Brett. Just once. Kiss me."

He briefly closed his eyes, then gave in. His lips pushed hard against hers and then eased to seduce them soft and open. Her heartbeat slammed against her breast as she felt him enter her mouth with his tongue. Chills shivered down her skin, heat burned deep in her belly.

He lifted his head, his eyes a blazing-hot blue. "You're a witch," he said.

Maybe so. Because inside her, confidence built and the dragon roared, adding to the sexual fire that she didn't bother hiding anymore.

She touched his face again, even more determined. "Now that we've done the teenage stuff, I thought we could grow up," she said, her voice surprisingly steady as she laid it straight on the line. "I thought you might make love to me."

I THOUGHT YOU MIGHT make love to me.

Brett couldn't get the words out of his head, even

though the minute she'd uttered them he'd slid her off his lap and instructed the driver to take them back to the apartment complex pronto.

She looked at him now, eyebrows raised, as if still waiting for him to answer the question.

He scrubbed a hand over his face. "Don't even think about it."

A little smile curved her lips. "If you're talking to me, it's *way* too late."

She bent over to retrieve the champagne flute that had fallen to the floor and set it in one of the built-in holders. Her hair had half fallen from its knot and trailed down her back. Smooth and silky, it curled against the sheer pink fabric, and he wanted to touch the stuff, then touch her skin, then do to her all the things she didn't know she was asking for when she'd said, *I thought you might make love to me*.

She took up a fresh glass. "Some champagne, please?" she said, holding it out to him. The chilled bottle was on his side of the limousine.

"No!" Somebody needed a clear head, and his was more than muddled.

She frowned and reached across him to grasp the bottle herself. "It's perfectly legal."

He pressed back against his seat so her arm wouldn't brush him. "Well you shouldn't be," he muttered.

Champagne glug-glugged into her glass. "I heard

that,'' she said, then lifted her glass in his direction. Her gaze captured his. "To us," she said.

He couldn't look away. Like static electricity, sex still crackled in the air, and he called himself every son-of-a-curse he could think of for starting on this path to disaster.

She took a swallow of champagne. It was the kind of swallow that loosened inhibitions, and he edged farther away from her.

"You haven't answered the question," she said.

"You couldn't have been serious." There. That said it all. That said they'd been playing around. Flirting. Enjoying a little male-female game that didn't need to go anywhere beyond the few kisses they'd shared.

He didn't let himself think of the sweet, heated taste of her mouth.

"I am serious."

He thought about jumping out of the car. Anything to end this conversation. He'd wanted to restore her confidence, not create a whopper of a problem for himself.

"Hah." He thought it sounded a little like a laugh.

"Hah?" She repeated, then drained her champagne. "Are you afraid you won't respect me in the morning?"

"I'm afraid I won't respect *me* in the morning," he muttered, then stopped, appalled at how that had sounded and by the stunned look on her face. "No, no, you don't understand. That didn't come out right."

He slid closer to her. He found himself taking the champagne glass from her and then holding her hands in his. "How could I...take this from you, Francesca?" He brought her fingers up to his mouth and kissed them, like a supplicant asking for royal favors.

He felt the fine tremble in her hands, and she shook her head. "Why can't it be something I *give* to you?"

"Francesca. Your family would kill me."

She stubbornly set her chin. "This is not about them. This is about *me*."

He sighed.

Then she withdrew her fingers from his. She turned sideways on the wide bench seat to face him fully and placed her hands on his shoulders. The small and warm touch roller-coasted to his toes.

"Who taught me to ride a bike?" she said.

He thought back. "I guess...I did."

"Who showed me how to make a kite tail and wind the string on a stick?"

He frowned. "Me."

"Who held my hand when I ice-skated the first time, and who made sure I didn't throw like a girl, and who taught me how to dive instead of belly flop?"

She'd tackled each new skill with a verve and intensity that he'd admired even as a teenager. She'd had a passion— Damn.

Passion.

Brett closed his eyes, but she kept talking, whispering like the temptation she was turning out to be.

"You, you, you," Francesca said. "You were there every time I needed to learn something new."

She wanted a teacher, a tutor, a mentor, in…sex. But she'd call it lovemaking and right there was the biggest sticking point.

Maybe she could read the objection on his face. ''I'm not asking for forever, Brett. I'm asking you for tonight. I want this and I trust you. You'd never hurt me.''

But he might. He could. And her passion would definitely burn him. His blood pumped hot and heavy, and the sight of her naked torso flashed through his mind. He could almost feel the plump heat of her breasts against him.

Setting his back teeth, he took hold of her hands again and drew them off his shoulders. He cradled her fingers in his own. That's what he was supposed to be doing. Sheltering her, protecting her, not remembering the taste of her skin or the responsive catch of her breath.

The limo rolled to a stop. Brett looked out the window and realized they'd made it back to the apartments. Just in time. He'd say no as gently as he could, and she wouldn't have a chance to work those wiles of hers on him again.

He opened his mouth.

But she spoke first. ''Think about it, Brett. If it's not you, it *will* be someone else.''

At the words, the burn in his blood and his belly turned to red fire in his brain.

Scruples fled. Reasons not to involve himself retreated. Every rational thought receded, and everything but Francesca turned hazy dark.

He slipped his hands from her fingers to handcuff one of her wrists. He pulled her from the car, dug money from his pocket and tossed it at the driver. Walking as quickly as he could, he led her in the direction of his apartment. One part of his brain realized she was almost running to keep up.

The rest of his brain just wanted to be alone with her as soon as possible.

In seconds they were inside. In an instant he'd slammed shut the door. He didn't bother with the lights. Surrounded by inky blackness he pushed Francesca back against the door and dove for the dark heat of her mouth.

He thought he heard her gasp, but he didn't let up. He pressed harder, pressed forward, pushing his tongue into her mouth and taking her taste into himself.

If it's not you it will *be someone else.*

When he couldn't breathe, he lifted his head and breathed raggedly. "Well?" he said hoarsely. "Sex isn't kites and bike rides. I can't be gentle with you, Francesca. Not every moment. Not even if I wanted to."

He closed his eyes, and his heartbeat pounded like flashes of fire against his eyelids.

If it's not you it will *be someone else.*

His breaths moved harshly in and out of his lungs. "It's now or never, Francesca." He stepped away from her, every muscle in his body granite hard. "Your call."

Only one more quick breath passed. Then she came against him, her arms around his neck, her mouth hot against his throat. "Now," she said, her voice strained with what he recognized as passion. His skin shuddered in response. "Please, Brett. Now."

DESPITE her big brave words and the tingling desire in her body, an armada of goose bumps set sail down Francesca's spine. She'd expected Brett to be a tender and gentle lover, but he was hot and hard, and she was a little afraid she couldn't keep up with him.

She bit down on her lower lip, but then he was there instead, seducing her with a heavy, heated kiss. Her limbs went soft, and she locked her arms around his neck to stay upright.

"That's right," he said, his voice hoarse and deep. "Lean against me, honey. I want to feel you."

Francesca shuddered in response, and he trailed his mouth down her neck. He kissed her there, too, and she almost fainted at the sweet, slight burn of his whiskers.

His mouth returned to her lips. "Kiss me back," he murmured to her, but she couldn't. She couldn't kiss or say his name or even breathe, because his fingers found the zipper at the back of her dress and in seconds he'd opened it and peeled the dress from her shoulders. The fabric pooled at her feet and he dragged her out of the tangle of its folds by stepping back.

"Let me feel you," he said again, his voice harsh, his hands hot and hurried as they trailed down her shoulders to her wrists. She still wore a strapless bra and panties and yet Brett's touch was so knowing, so intimate, so *impatient* that her heart sped up again and she gasped for air.

He took her mouth again but she wrenched her face away because she needed still more time to breathe. His heart pounded insistently against her chest, and when he lifted her against him, pushing her hips against his so his arousal pressed against the notch at her thighs, she felt a sob rise.

He didn't seem to notice her panic. He twisted his head and thrust his tongue into her mouth and she stiffened, instinctively pushing away from him with her hands.

He didn't seem to notice that, either, instead grinding his pelvis against hers and kissing her neck.

"Brett."

Tears stung the corners of her eyes and a real sob tore through her throat. "Brett, *please*. Stop."

Instantly he drew his hips away from hers. Instantly his hands softened and loosened. "Have you had enough?" he asked quietly.

"Uh…" She blinked in confusion and a now-extraneous tear burned a path down her cheek. "Wh-what?"

He moved completely away from her, and she followed the sound of his voice toward his living room couch. "Have you had enough?" he repeated.

With the back of her hand she wiped her face dry. "I…I don't get it."

"Damn it, Francesca." His voice sounded strained.

"You must be careful what you ask for. Be careful *who* you ask for."

She came several steps forward. "Are you saying I should be afraid of you?"

"No. Yes." In the darkness she could barely make out the wave of his hand. "Maybe this is one of those things that come with the experience of prom dates and making out in cars. You've just got to learn to be more careful about offering yourself."

A flush of embarrassment heated her cheeks. "So that—" she pointed toward the door "—that was about teaching me a lesson?"

"You wanted to learn, didn't you?" he said flatly. "And if not from me, from someone else. Well, that's what somebody else might offer you."

Francesca had never been a cryer and didn't think that now would be a good time to start, but she felt a new sting of tears nonetheless. "You scared me." In the darkness she stared at Brett accusingly. "You really scared me."

Silence welled in his side of the room. Then his voice sounded, hard and cool. "That was the whole point, Francesca."

Anger moved in to replace the tears, and Francesca welcomed it. She stomped over to her dress and stepped inside, then wriggled to pull it over her hips. "Well, thank you very much, but I'm not an idiot."

From his side of the room there was a grumble.

She sent a murderous glare his way. "I'm *not* acting

like one. An idiot *would* go to any man when she wanted to make love for the first time. An idiot *would* have found a way when she was sixteen or eighteen or twenty or anytime before now, if all she wanted was to have sex.''

She heard his quick intake of breath.

''Well, I'm smarter than that. I'm smart enough to wait until I'm ready. I'm smart enough to pick a man that I…care about. A man who makes my skin quiver and my bones melt and who I *thought* I could count on to make me feel beautiful. To make *it* beautiful.''

She struggled with the zipper that seemed stuck somewhere at the small of her back. ''If you ask *me* Brett, the only stupid one around here is *you.*''

The zipper wouldn't budge. She wanted to stamp her foot in frustration, but that would take precious seconds away from a timely exit. She just had to get this dress on! Arms behind her, she worked at the dress, feeling the shoulder straps slide down her naked shoulders.

The light beside the couch blazed on.

She stood there, caught in its glare, half angry, half teary and half-dressed. Three halves, she thought hysterically. That can't be right.

''Francesca.''

She didn't want to look at him. She didn't want to see any smugness or superiority on his face. The zipper moved an inch, stuck again.

''Francesca, please. Look at me.''

She breathed out her nose impatiently. "What?" she said, reluctantly sliding her gaze in his direction.

The light from the lamp colored his hair gold, and he'd tossed off his jacket and tie. His white shirt was open at the throat, and his blue eyes took hold of hers and wouldn't let go. "I'm sorry," he said. "I screwed up and I'm sorry."

Her hands froze on the zipper. He had an expression on his face she'd never seen before. His cheekbones pushed starkly against his skin and his eyes were wide and serious. "I don't know if I wished you hadn't grown up or I'm down-on-my-knees grateful you did or…" He shook his head. "I just can't seem to get this right."

He rose from the couch and walked toward her. "Let me help you, honey." With achingly gentle hands he turned her so her back was to him. She let go of the zipper and he eased it up, past her hips, her waist, the middle of her back.

"There," he said. "All done."

She didn't turn around.

He didn't move.

And then he touched his mouth to her shoulder. Gently. A butterfly's kiss that made Francesca's nipples harden and warmth pool instantly between her legs.

Oh.

He rested his cheek against the top of her head and pulled her back against him. His shirtfront was scratchy and hot, and her skin rose in goose bumps to meet it.

"Let me, Francesca?" His voice was soft and hoarse at the same time. "Let me try again?"

8

BENEATH HIS HANDS Brett felt Francesca tremble. He'd made her afraid and he hated himself for it. She was beautiful and sweet and fragile, and if he didn't restore her faith in him he wouldn't forgive himself.

He kissed the side of her neck, gently, softly, closing his eyes to the seductive scent of her perfume, remembering how she'd tried it out on him that first night.

For better or worse, she wanted him. And the only thought he could focus on now was making sure it was better. The best.

"Francesca?" he murmured against her skin. "Let me have another chance?"

The stiffness slowly flowed out of her body. "Admit you're an idiot," she said.

"I'm an idiot." He sucked lightly on the side of her neck.

Her voice came fainter. "And you were wrong."

"I'm often wrong." He breathed against her temple and she shivered.

"And…and…" She leaned back lightly against him and shivered again. "I'm nervous."

He squeezed her shoulders, half relieved, half disappointed. "Then why don't we say good-night."

"*No!*" Her body straightened and she took a quick breath. "Sorry. Sorry. Just feeling a bit skittish."

"Are you sure—"

"I'm sure!"

Brett pressed his fingers against her shoulders, kneading the tight muscles. "Then just relax. Think of tonight as…"

"As what?" Her muscles remained tensed. "A rite of passage? An initiation rite?"

"Yeah," he said softly and smiled. "To probably the world's biggest club."

She didn't laugh.

Brett continued massaging her shoulders. If she was determined to go through with this, he was determined to make it worthwhile. No mechanical, let's-get-it-over-with act for Francesca.

"Speaking of clubs." He put his mouth against her ear. "Remember when you wanted to join our Boys Only Club?"

Her lips curved up. "My brothers refused. They would have broken your legs if they knew you let me into that rickety clubhouse you built in our backyard."

Brett wondered briefly what punishment they'd enact if they knew what he was doing now, then pushed the thought away. "That's right," he said. "I took you out there and showed you the place."

Her body leaned back against his. "In the middle of the night."

"I bet it wasn't much later than nine, but okay."

Francesca shook her head and her hair tickled his chin. "You said it had to be pitch-black."

Brett slid a glance in the direction of the living room lamp. "I did, didn't I?" In an instant he strode to the light, turned it off and returned to Francesca. "I remember now. You'd been bugging me about it all day. I said we had to wait until dark."

In the blackness inside his apartment, he heard her breathing quicken. Then he knelt by her feet.

"What are you doing?"

"Don't you remember?" he said, circling her ankle to lift one foot. "So we wouldn't get caught creeping out of the house you had to take off your shoes."

She didn't protest. Having taken both her shoes off, he stood. Then he reached around her back, the tab of the zipper cool against the hot skin of his fingers.

Francesca jerked. "Wh-what?"

He pulled it down. "Someone might hear the rustle of your clothes," he said matter-of-factly, the escapade of the past turning into another kind of game entirely. "We better take them off."

The *bzzzip* of the zipper opening sounded loud and harsh in the darkness. Brett's pulse started a sledgehammer beat, and he swallowed hard as the dress fell away from her. He leaned down to kiss the side of her neck, stroking the spot with his tongue.

She moaned.

"Shh," he said, moving upward toward her ear. "We have to be very, very quiet."

At her sides, he laced their fingers and just leaned into her, letting her become accustomed to the heat and hardness of his body.

"What about your clothes?" she whispered. Strained tension remained in her voice.

He ignored the question and instead lifted her light form into his arms. "The grass is wet on the way to the clubhouse. And because you're afraid of slugs—"

"I am *not* afraid of slugs!"

"And because you're afraid of frogs—"

"Frogs, either!"

Smiling, he turned toward the short hallway. "And because you're a kind young woman you'll indulge me and let me carry you to the clubhouse." Inside his bedroom, he shut the door behind them with a *snick*.

It was cool and even darker than the living room. Brett slid Francesca down his body, then held her lightly against him. "What do you think of the place?"

"As I recall there was nothing but a dirt floor and the stub of a candle." She was talking about the old clubhouse.

"That's because I'd hid the stack of girlie magazines."

There was real shock in Francesca's voice. "No!"

He shrugged. "Well, I think we had a couple of pages of ladies underwear ads torn from the Sears catalog."

She giggled. "You didn't."

"I'll never tell." The truth didn't matter. What mattered was that Francesca was relaxed against him and laughing.

She sighed. "You were very nice to me, you know."

He drew a forefinger from her wrist to her bare shoulder. "I was, wasn't I? Didn't I even go so far as to spill all the details of our secret ceremonies?" His finger traced across her collarbone and he felt her tremble.

"You even initiated me," she said.

His fingers drifted toward the top curves of her generous breasts. "I did, didn't I?"

Then she went serious and quiet and with calm intent he picked her up again and strode the few feet to his bed. He pushed aside the down comforter and laid Francesca against the cool sheets. He stretched out beside her.

"That initiation rite involved blood," she said.

"Just a little." As he remembered, he'd pricked her ring finger with a pin. "And I didn't hurt you."

"No," Francesca replied. "You never hurt me."

He hoped he wouldn't now, either. He leaned across her. "I'm going to turn the light on."

She grabbed his arm. "I thought you said we needed to be in the dark."

"But we're safe inside now, Francesca." And he needed to be able to see her face. He needed to gauge her reaction to his next move. To his every move. Because he never wanted to scare her again. He only wanted to bring her pleasure.

The bedside light clicked on to provide a dim glow. Brett rolled back into place and then cast a glance at Francesca.

And nearly fell out of the bed.

"Honey..." It came out of his mouth, unbidden, uncontrolled. *Honey.* Honey was the color of Francesca's skin against the white sheets, yards of skin revealed by white, tiny, high-cut panties and a strapless bra.

Honey was the consistency of the thick desire infusing his bloodstream, making his heart beat harder to prevent him from expiring of arousal.

Honey was the sweet, sweet anticipation of having Francesca for himself.

Heart slamming in his chest, he flattened himself against the mattress and stared up at the ceiling.

"Brett?"

"What's the square root of 167? How about 673?" Maybe using his brain would slow down his body.

She sounded confused. "What? I'm not sure I ever knew."

Brett wasn't sure he was going to make it through the night. Not when the woman he was supposed to make a gentle, treasured memory with was turning him on so hard and fast that his hands were shaking and his blood was deserting his brain for his groin.

"Are you...am I...okay?"

He groaned at the tentative note in her voice. "Francesca, you're so okay that I'm bound to forget how inexperienced you are.''

The old sassy Francesca returned for a moment. She smiled. ''So let's forget that and go back to the 'I'm so okay' part.'' One of her fingers reached out and touched a button on his tuxedo shirt. ''There are parts of you that I think are okay, too.''

Afraid to touch her at the moment, he fisted his hands as she unbuttoned his shirt then spread the edges. Her breath sucked in as she looked at his bare chest, and then she swept her palm over his flesh.

His heart and his arousal leaped toward her.

''Honey.'' He rolled to lean over her. His lips found hers, and she immediately opened her lips for him as her arms went around his neck. The heat of her mouth matched the heat of his blood.

The kiss went on, hungry and deep, as one of his hands ran over the silky skin of her arm up to her shoulder. She trembled as he traced the top line of her strapless bra then followed it back again. On his next path he paused at the deep valley between her breasts and then slowly slid two fingers down between them.

She moaned into his mouth.

Her hot, fragrant skin cradled his fingers, and he thrust against the insides of her breasts, echoing the movement of his tongue into her mouth. Francesca moaned again and twisted her hips against him.

The sound of her passion, the sweet taste of her mouth, her soft heat against his knuckles burned all notions of caution from his head. Hooking his fingers into the bra, he tore down the cups to fully reveal her breasts.

He broke the kiss, heaving in air along with her. He looked down at what he'd exposed, her generous breasts peaked by nipples as pink and tight as the rosebuds on the corsage still binding her wrist. The hand with the flowers fluttered up.

''Don't,'' he said quickly, catching that hand. ''Let me look. You're so beautiful, Francesca.'' With a reverent touch, he circled one nipple.

''Brett?'' His name trembled from her lips.

''Yes,'' he answered. And knowing that she was asking for what he needed, he bent to take her into his mouth, licking the warm skin of her breast. Her body bowed, pressing against his mouth, and when he hollowed his cheeks to suck in her nipple, the scent of roses mingled with the scent of Francesca.

He shivered as her hand stroked his hair and cool rose petals brushed against his heated neck.

Desire pooled hotly in his groin and created an insistent ache at the small of his back. He slid one leg over Francesca's and felt her hands stripping him of his shirt as he moved to her other nipple. He bit it gently—he couldn't help himself—and he shivered again as she moaned, her voice hoarse and needy.

''Brett.''

She was aroused, too, and hungry, and now her hands moved insistently over his bare back. He lifted his head. ''Soon, baby, soon.''

With shaking hands he slid her panties down her legs and then kissed her breasts again as he stroked her belly and thighs, each time lingering longer at the apex. With each kiss, each stroke, he felt the languor overtake her body. Her legs relaxed and inched apart and he didn't hesitate to introduce his touch there. Light and sure, he pressed into her folds.

Hot.

Hot and ready for him. His head began to throb in time with his pulse. Francesca twisted under his touch, trying to get closer. He backed off for a moment, to make her wait, to make her crazy, to make her want him with the same intensity that was burning him.

"What is this?" she asked, her voice uncertain.

He pressed back into her, deeper this time, his finger encased sweetly and hotly, just like her breasts had held him. "This is passion," he said. "Are you ready?"

He knew she was. She was wet and swollen and now her legs were fully open for him. Her thumb brushed across one of his nipples and he jerked.

In a quick movement he withdrew from her body then shucked his pants and boxers, tossing aside shoes and socks and diving right back to Francesca. As gently as he could, he took a breast in his mouth and then touched her between her legs again, stretching her body with two fingers.

Her hips tilted up to his hand. "Francesca." He groaned and reached blindly for a condom from the drawer in the night table. She lifted on her elbows to watch him, her dark eyes heavy-lidded and her cheeks flushed.

Brett burned. His thigh muscles twitched as he kneeled between her legs. He pushed them wide, trying to stay gentle, trying to stay in control, but that darkness in her eyes was heady desire. Passion poured into his body like hot wine, and passion dictated he hold her thighs open with his palms so he could watch as he entered her.

Slowly entered her.

He felt the resistance, heard her quick breath, but then he looked into her eyes and the hot desire he saw there still matched his. "I want you, Francesca," he said. And he spiraled into the darkness as he pushed into her.

She cried out.

But then her body arched upward and the glitter of tears didn't cool the burning passion in her eyes.

"Okay?" he asked, gritting his teeth to remain controlled.

"You're inside me," she said. And there was wonder in her voice as one tear slid down her cheek.

He bent over to lick it away. "And you're inside me," he reassured her gently, not even certain what he meant, but certain it was true. Then he felt her inside muscles squeeze him tentatively, and then he had to move, forcing himself to be controlled and gentle. Over and over he thrust into her, watching closely as she wound tighter and tighter until it took just one quick press of his thumb and one long drive of his body to show them both how to turn Francesca into a woman.

FRANCESCA LAY curled against the cradle of Brett's body, working to catch her breath and trying to ignore a welling feeling of panic.

This wasn't going right!

Just minutes ago she'd made love to the man she'd always dreamed of. She was supposed to feel satisfied and satiated, triumphant and womanly, and she had, for several delicious moments. But now overwhelming her was embarrassment and awkwardness, not the least of which was caused by the fact that she was completely naked except for the strangling twist of strapless bra that was still caught about her rib cage.

There was something else going on, too, something deeper inside her that she didn't want to think about and that she had to get away from.

"Francesca?" Brett went on one elbow and peered into her face. "Are you okay?"

She'd be a *lot* better if she could think of a really clever way of dashing back to her apartment without having to look Brett in the eye. Preferably dressed in an enveloping terry cloth robe.

Her belly-flutters quickened. Darn those women's magazines! They contained plenty of articles on the morning after, but nothing on the *moments* after. Especially not the moments after with the man whose touch tantalized and terrified you at the same time. How was a woman supposed to survive such heartbreaking intimacy?

"Francesca?" he said again, his voice concerned.

She swallowed. "I'm fine," she said, hoping she sounded cheerful and casual. "Right as rain. All in one piece."

One of his big hands stroked her shoulder. "Not quite."

A wash of heat spread over Francesca's face and those panic-flutters became out-and-out beating wings of anxiety. Yes. The irrevocable had happened here. And she wanted desperately to hightail it back in her apartment and hide from all the new feelings.

She eyed the distance from bed to the bedroom door. How was she supposed to manage a dignified exit? With her dress in the living room she'd have to skip out of Brett's room wearing only her bare backside and this devil-possessed bra. Her gaze caught on the bedside lamp. At least turn that off first. Darkness could only help.

She inched away from the warm curve of his body toward the cool expanse of the sheets, her movement rolling the errant bra into a tighter twist.

Brett put his hand on her arm. "Where are you going?"

She froze, his fingers burning her with the kind of heat that sent a field of goose bumps blooming across her body. *Someplace where I can think. Somewhere away from your touch.*

She swallowed. "Just thought I'd turn the light off."

"Let me."

A hope that he'd get out of the bed to accomplish the task, leaving her to remove the bra unnoticed, was born and died in the same instant as he leaned across her. His chest flattened her shoulders against the mattress, then with a click the light in the room changed. Except not to blessed darkness.

No, the golden glow of the lamp was replaced by the silver shine of moonlight spilling through the bedroom's high window.

Oh, great. Because that silvery light meant that when she ran away from him she'd be flashing one bright moon herself.

Her breath strangled again as she tried to come up with a plan. If she could just get the darn bra off! If worse came to worst she'd look better leaving the room naked than leaving it tied up in a piece of underwear.

Inspiration struck. "Could I—could you get me a drink of water, please?"

"Sure."

Francesca held her breath. When Brett disappeared into the adjoining bathroom she could race to the living room for her dress.

Instead, he headed in the direction of the living room himself.

"Where are you going?" she asked quickly.

He paused at the foot of the bed, naked and unconcerned. "Water," he said. "And glasses. They're in the kitchen. Anything else?"

Francesca shook her head because she couldn't speak. The moonlight silvered the angles of Brett's body. Staring at the wide strength of his shoulders and the hard angles of his hip bones caused her mouth to go dry. She kept shaking her head.

After he left the room it took her a couple of seconds to collect herself. Then, with a mental slap to her forehead, she jackknifed into a sitting position and began to attack the bra. At least she could divest herself of that problem.

Fingers fumbling in haste, she tried working the twisted strip of fabric around her body to reach the hooks. The darn bra seemed pasted to her rib cage and she broke into a cold sweat. Which, of course, made the stretchy material stick to her skin even closer.

Just when she was wishing she was limber enough to attack the thing with her teeth, Brett's voice sounded.

"You need some help?"

Francesca froze again, even though she was horribly aware of how she must look, sheets tumbled about her waist, everything above bare and propped up by a twist of fabric that wouldn't let go.

It was all too much.

The anticipation of the evening, the sexual tension, the "lesson" Brett had tried to teach her, the experience he *had* shared with her. All too much. Tears stung Francesca's eyes and to her everlasting mortification she had to place her hands over her face to staunch the flow.

Brett swore.

And even before one tear could roll to her chin, she found herself in his arms. "Baby," he said. He was warm and his heartbeat thumped reassuringly strong beneath her cheek. "Don't cry."

She hiccuped. "Not crying," she said, her face buried against him. "It's just that your shoulder is wet."

He stroked her hair with his hand. "You're right. It's all my fault."

"Yes." From within the circle of his arms, nothing seemed quite so terrible. "You should have taken off my bra."

He didn't laugh. "You're right," he said, and she almost instantly felt relief as he reached down and quickly released the hooks. "Better?" he asked.

She nodded, rubbing her face against his skin to dry the last of her tears.

He continued to stroke her hair and his other palm swept across her back. In a hoarse whisper he spoke soothing words against the top of her head.

Francesca relaxed, melting into the warmth of his body. With the embarrassing bra situation handled, it didn't seem so imperative she go home right away. Though there was still some nervousness, some knowledge, flopping around deep in her belly, she could ignore it as long as Brett touched her with his sure, tantalizing fingers.

She blew out a deep sigh and Brett tilted up her face with a hand under her chin. He kissed her wet eyelashes and then her nose—sweet kisses of understanding.

Francesca's stomach went full-blown panicky again.

"Okay?" he asked, smiling down at her.

Déjà vu. She'd been here before. Or probably dreamed this moment. Naked in Brett's arms, his smile warm and knowing after their night together. But the dream couldn't hold a candle to the sweet burning fire of reality.

Her stomach roiled again, the walls behind Brett tilted dizzily, she put one hand against the mattress to prevent her whole world from toppling over.

Then the movement stopped—stomach, walls, Brett, world settling into a new order.

"Better?" he asked.

No. She smiled back, though, wide enough to show her molars. Because there couldn't be any more tears. Nothing even close.

Brett had given her the night together she'd asked for. The one she said would satisfy her. *I'm not asking for forever.* She'd said those very words.

But here in his arms, warm and comfortable and comforted, she couldn't ignore the truth that had been rolling around in her stomach all night. The truth that had nothing to do with twisted bras or bare-naked embarrassment.

The bare-naked truth was she loved him. She was *in love* with him.

That she wanted forever with Brett.

9

BAM! BAM! BAM! The banging on his front door woke Brett.

Blinking, it took him a few moments to orient himself. Weak sunlight washed into his bedroom. Francesca was in his arms, her face pressed into the hollow of his shoulder.

Morning already. The last he remembered, she'd fallen asleep, all damp eyelashes and warm skin. He'd held her, watching her breathe for hours, vigilant against another flurry of uncharacteristic tears.

Bam! Bam! Bam! More banging. Francesca's eyes fluttered open.

"Yo! Brett!" A deep voice reached all the way to the bedroom.

"Oh, my God." Francesca immediately sat up, clutching the sheet to her throat. "Oh, my God, it's Carlo."

Brett reached out to push a tendril of hair off her cheek. "Don't worry. The front door is locked."

The banging resumed and Francesca pushed on his shoulder. "You've got to go answer him."

"No way." He and Francesca needed to talk about what had happened between them last night. He wanted to know exactly why she'd cried and what they were going to do now.

The banging started again.

Francesca's eyes widened. "Brett!"

"Okay, okay, I'll get rid of him." He slipped out of bed and slipped into his boxers, then tripped over Francesca's shoes on his way to the front door.

Leaning against the cool wood he called through it to his friend. "Carlo! What do you want?"

There was a pause, then Carlo's voice, puzzled. "You're not going to let me in?"

"Give me a break. I just woke up. *You* just woke me up."

More silence. "Fine. Whatever. Want to shoot some hoops? Then we'll go for a heart-attack-on-a-plate breakfast at Judy's Diner."

Brett opened his mouth to refuse. He should take Francesca out for brunch. At a small table in some quiet place where they could talk through what had happened.

From the corner of his eye he saw something move. Francesca, creeping into the living room wearing only her panties and bra. On tiptoe, she dashed over to her dress and snatched it from the floor.

"Brett! What do you say? Hoops and a heart attack?"

He figured he already had the heart attack covered, seeing Francesca in her skimpy underthings again. "N—"

"Say yes!" Francesca hissed. "If you say no he'll suspect something."

Brett continued to stare at her, her words failing to register. Not when her hair was mussed and her lips were red from his kisses and he could see the pink scrape of his beard against her neck.

"Say yes," she whispered.

"Brett!" Carlo again.

He turned his head toward the door. "Give me a second," he called out. Then he turned back to Francesca. "We need to talk," he whispered back, his mind made stupid again by everything that had entranced him the night before. Every bit of her.

Francesca shook her head. "No, we don't. I asked you for last night. End of story."

"End of story?"

"What?" Carlo yelled through the door. "Are you talking to me?"

Francesca bit her lip. "I *told* you I didn't want forever." She stepped into her dress and struggled with the zipper.

Brett started toward her but she waved him off. "Thanks, by the way," she said.

Thanks, by the way? "We've *got* to talk."

"Then talk to Carlo." She slipped on her sandals. "Promise me you can keep him occupied at the front here so I can go out your back door and into mine."

Brett remembered that Carlo's apartment was between his and Francesca's. Thank God he hadn't thought of it until now. Double thank God that his bedroom was on the other side of the apartment and didn't share a wall with Carlo.

"Brett? Are you okay in there?"

Francesca's eyes widened. "Tell him yes."

But how could he when he wasn't sure it was true? He needed to talk things over with Francesca. Think things through. Taste her mouth again before she walked away. "Really, Fr—"

"Shh!" She took a step, frowned, slipped back out of her shoes. "You're invited to that party for Elise and David tonight, right? We can talk there."

"Brett, ol' buddy. My detective antennae are quivering." Carlo's teasing voice came through the door. "You got a body in there?"

Francesca sent Brett a panicked look and then ran barefooted toward his back door. "Let him in and keep him busy for a few minutes," she whispered one last time.

In seconds she'd eased out of his apartment. Brett opened the front door, running his hand through his hair and aware it took zero acting skill for him to appear stupid and confused and like a guy who'd just been woken from the middle of a particularly luscious dream.

"What's going on?" Carlo said by way of greeting, stepping inside.

Brett wished he knew.

FRANCESCA WAS the first guest to arrive at the barbecue Elise's parents were giving for the almost-married couple. When Elise had lost the battle for a small wedding, her parents had promised an early, more casual celebration for them.

In a pretty sundress, Elise took one look at Francesca's khaki pants, plain white blouse tied at the waist and baseball cap, then hauled her out to the far reaches of the backyard beyond anyone's hearing. "What happened?" she asked. "Besides disaster."

Francesca tugged her ball cap lower and shoved her hands in her pockets. "I made a mistake."

Elise narrowed her eyes. "I'm going to kill him. Better yet, I'll tell your brothers and they'll kill him."

"Don't. It's my fault and my fault only."

Elise sighed. "You're head-over-heels, aren't you?"

"And out of my league." Francesca scuffed the toe of her thick fisherman's sandal against the grass. "But it's over with. I'm going back to stick-in-the-mud Francesca. Out of those stupid dresses and back into my jeans."

"That's not going to mend your heart."

"But I'll be a heck of a lot more comfortable." Francesca tried pasting on a grin. "C'mon. Take me to your leader. Your mom will find something to distract me."

Francesca volunteered for pass duty. Wandering through the party, toting large platters of hors d'oeuvres, gave her a good reason to see everybody and linger long with nobody. Bean dip dabs on round tortilla chips, celery packed with cream cheese and salsa, spicy miniature *taquitos,* she blessed them all as she chose who to offer them to and what group to avoid.

When Brett arrived she zipped into the kitchen and spent several minutes refilling the largest platter. After a deep breath she returned to the patio and started circulating again. So what if the group of men Brett was with didn't get a chance at the appetizers. None of them really appeared very hungry.

Well, Brett kind of did. He managed to catch her eye as she made a wide circle around him and the others standing beside the cooler filled with microbrewed beers. The expression on his face, intent and determined, made the little hairs on her neck, the ones right beneath the ponytail she'd shoved through her baseball cap, stand up.

She tugged the brim of her cap lower and ducked in the opposite direction to make another unnecessary platter refill.

As she came out of the kitchen he was there, though, and caught her arm. She pinned on a bright smile. ''Hors d'oeuvre? *Taquito?*''

He didn't look down at her proffered plate. ''Talk,'' he said.

She raised her eyebrows. ''I've been conscripted to kitchen duty. Can't really desert until, um, after dessert.''

He ignored her pun. ''When are we going to talk?''

The touch of his fingers on her upper arm tingled—

hot little pinpricks of response that tightened her nipples and made the flesh across her stomach twitch.

He shook her arm a little. "When, Francesca?"

Several months. Several years, maybe. Sometime when remembering Brett's chest under her palms, Brett's mouth on her breasts, Brett *inside* her, wouldn't freeze dry her tongue, making speech nearly impossible.

"I—" She tried moistening her lips. "Look, couldn't we just leave it alone?"

He flattened his mouth. "You mean leave you alone."

She didn't think she should agree. "Do we really need to rehash the event, Brett? I'm fine. You look okay. What more is there?"

He frowned. "I don't like this casual attitude of yours."

Men. Francesca let out a gusty sigh. "Great, then. When are we getting married?"

Astonishment widened his eyes and dropped his jaw.

The full plate of appetizers was getting heavy. "Here," she said, offering the food again. "Stuff something in that wide mouth of yours."

"Francesca—"

"Please, Brett, give me some credit. I was just kidding. I know exactly where you're coming from. I've lived with men my entire life, okay?"

He crossed his arms over his chest. "And what has that experience taught you, O Small-but-wise One?"

"You males put extremely high value on your piles of dirty socks and your meals of microwave burritos and the freedom to drop everything for beers and billiards with the boys. It requires a kind of atomic explosion to blast you out of bachelorhood.''

He shifted uncomfortably. ''Atomic explosion?''

She shrugged. ''You tell me.'' She nodded her head in the direction of Elise, standing nearby with her fiancé at her side. ''With David there, it's clear. He's completely besotted and they love each other in a way that's explosive itself.''

Brett glanced at the engaged couple. ''That might just burn out.''

''I'll lay odds that it won't.''

Brett's gaze sharpened. ''Francesca, you may think you know—''

''Franny!'' A male Milano voice sounded from across the grass. ''We're hungry over here!''

Francesca looked over at the knot of brothers beckoning to her. ''I *do* know, Brett. And you, you're a special case. Rebachelored,'' she said flippantly. ''A guy like you will be eating out of the microwave for the rest of his life.''

Or, Francesca thought, he'll find himself bowled over by some paragon of poised femininity like Patricia. A woman who knew how to dress and how to make love and how not to blubber like a baby when she thought she'd never be held by him again.

''Franny!'' The Milanos yelled as one.

She pivoted obediently toward the hungry-brother bellow, grateful she had an excuse to get away before she said something really dumb. "I'm done with the subject."

Maybe attorneys had to have the last word. Maybe it was men in general. Because Brett called out to her as she walked away.

"Perfect," he said. "Because then you'll just listen when it's my turn."

FULL OF STEAK, salad and corn on the cob, Brett sat back in a cushioned patio chair and watched Francesca wander over to one corner of the deep backyard. A basketball hoop reigned at one end of a cement half court and she unearthed a basketball from beneath a bordering shrub and started shooting aimless baskets.

For a short person, and a girl, she was a pretty good shot. She talked a pretty good game, too.

Bachelors. Rebachelors. He shook his head. She thought she had it all down pat.

But if he knew what was good for him he'd leave things just as she'd left them. He would feel relieved that she was willing to let their one-night stand, well, stand, and not need to take it any further.

But his protective instinct wasn't so easily slayed.

He'd been trying to kill it all evening.

Like a mythical beast, though, it rose again and again, prodding him with sharp talons each time she spoke with another man. Each time he heard her laugh.

And though he cursed himself for all kinds of a fool, while she'd been passing plates around he hadn't been able to get the image out of his head of Francesca passing herself to another man—now that he'd taken the first bite.

He suppressed a groan, thinking of her beneath him the night before. She'd cried out when he'd entered her body, but once the pain had left her face, something had infused him, some *power* that he didn't dare examine.

He scraped his hands over his face. There was a fine line between protectiveness and possessiveness and he *must* keep on the right side of it.

The vow didn't keep him from narrowing his gaze at the man who this minute was approaching Francesca. Brett recognized him as the driver who'd dropped her off a few nights before.

She stopped dribbling. Smiled at the guy.

The other man said something, grinning, too. He pantomimed making a basket.

Francesca pulled a face and put one hand on her hip.

They both laughed.

Brett could read their next exchange in the body language. A challenge was issued. A challenge was accepted. A little game of one-on-one.

Innocent. Fun. But still Brett found himself half rising from his chair as Francesca dropped the basketball to start unbuttoning her shirt. He slumped back once he could see the white tank top she wore underneath. Then she completely shed the overshirt to reveal the golden skin of her arms that last night she'd wound around his neck. Brett's blood began to chug heavily through his body.

Her shirt was tossed over a nearby shrub. She let the guy take the basketball out first. Brett realized the other man needed the advantage. He was a lousy shot.

Or maybe just a calculating one. Because he allowed Francesca to control the ball most of their game while he did a foul-worthy job of defending the basket. Chest out, he tried using his bigger size to intimidate her. Or maybe he was using every excuse to brush up against her.

The game ended quickly, though. His tomboy princess won, and acknowledged her opponent's congratulations with a curtsy. Brett found himself smiling.

But then he saw a second challenge being issued and he could tell how easily Francesca rose to the bait. That was her MO, and exactly how Carlo enticed her into that bridesmaid's bet.

Blood chugging hot and heavy again, Brett popped out of his seat. He hustled toward the court, ignoring the stiffness already settling in his muscles from his own play with Carlo that morning. That damned bet couldn't be ignored. And he worried, now that she'd booted him out of the picture, that Francesca would be looking for some way to beat Carlo.

She liked to win.

But so did Brett.

The basketball rested on the cement beside Francesca's feet. He reached it for it, grabbed it up. She stared at him, blinking.

"I'm playing the winner," he announced.

"We just agreed on another game," the other guy said. "You'll be up next."

Brett wasn't in the mood to talk. "My turn," he told Francesca. "Now."

"Hey," the loser protested. "She just agreed to double or nothing."

Brett's whole body went tight. "What're the stakes?" he asked Francesca.

She frowned at him. "I don't think—"

"What are the stakes?"

"For goodness sake, Brett. Pizza. We're betting pizzas."

Yeah, and he could just picture it. An intimate booth in a dark Italian restaurant. Francesca's cheeks flushed and her lips the color of red wine and this…this…*loser* sharing a pizza with her and then sharing her bed later.

"Never gonna happen," he told the guy.

"What?"

"Never gonna happen." Brett eyed him implacably. *"This is my game."*

The guy looked at Brett, looked at Francesca, looked back at Brett again. Then he held up his hands in surrender. "Got it." With a good-natured grin he headed back to the rest of the party.

Smart man. Brett liked him better already.

He turned toward Francesca. Her hands were back on

her hips. Her tank top clung damply to her slender rib cage and lush breasts. Lust pierced him like a sword.

''What's this all about?'' she said, her eyes spitting dark fire at him. ''You're acting very strange.''

He shook his head. Strange would be letting her get away now. With only a few days left until the wedding, she'd be looking for a way to win that bet. And the only one who was going to help her do that was him.

He dribbled the ball a few times. ''I don't like playing for pizzas.''

''Fine.'' She crossed her arms over her chest. ''We'll play for honor.''

Bomp. Bomp. Bomp. The ball echoed the loud thump of his heartbeat. ''No. Something else.'' He didn't want to think about honor right now.

She frowned. ''What then? What's going on, Brett?''

A bead of sweat rolled from her temple down her cheek, mesmerizing him. Damn. Tempting him.

Stepping toward her, he caught the drop on his thumb. Then he brought his thumb to his mouth and licked off her taste.

Sweet. Salty. Francesca.

Her eyes widened and she swallowed. ''Brett?''

''We'll play to eleven,'' he said. ''When I win, you'll come back to my bed tonight.''

It wasn't a bad idea, he thought. It would keep her occupied. It would keep him sane.

FRANCESCA COULD HAVE refused to play under such outrageous conditions. She could have walked off the court.

Instead, she negotiated for a six-point lead.

She hadn't been raised to back down.

But as the game began, she wasn't sure if winning wasn't really losing.

Brett wanted her. It was in the intent look on his face, the harsh intake of his breath, the very real bump he gave her with his hip as she feinted around him.

Shoot. *Swish.* One basket and she had seven points to his zero.

Her lead didn't faze him. He drove the ball toward the basket, and Francesca tried to move in front of him, her heart banging under the triple threat of adrenaline, confusion, desire.

He made four points in a row.

Breathing hard, she still didn't know who she rooted for—herself or her childhood hero.

Though he wasn't playing heroically. Or gentlemanly, either. He grunted when he made another basket and then drilled the ball toward her, a chest pass that stung when it hit her palms.

His intensity was half scary, half exhilarating. Giddy with excitement, her next shot bounced off the rim, but she was quicker than he was and grabbed the rebound. She dribbled, trying to position herself in that personal sweet spot from which she nearly always made a basket.

Brett was in front of her. Between the last points, he'd thrown off his shirt, and the sheen of sweat on his chest distracted her. She hesitated, he closed in and she closed her eyes, shooting blindly.

Swish. Eight to five.

The play turned even more serious. Brett started a verbal—and titillating—form of distraction.

"I'm going to have you tonight," he said.

Her shot went wild.

He picked up the ball and closed the gap in their scores. He had nine. She managed to get her points to ten.

"And there won't be any reason to cry," he said, his eyes glittering blue as she passed him the ball.

She didn't like him assuming she would be so easy— to have and to please. Let him work a little harder for both.

She gritted her teeth and focused on the ball. *Get it back,* she commanded herself. There was pride involved here. More than pride. Her heart. But he was quick and strong, and too soon it was ten points to ten.

She missed her next chance. Brett got the ball again, but she shut out everything but the orange orb and used the last of her energy reserves to bat it out of Brett's hands.

Sucking in air, she lifted the ball for her shot. This was it. Her confidence surged. She knew she could best him. "You're gonna owe me pizza," she said, grinning and sparing him a glance.

He stood back, silent, until the instant the ball left her hands. "I'm gonna make you scream," he said.

Her follow-through failed. The ball sputtered in the air. Brett grabbed it, made his own shot, swift and sure.

Swish.

He wiped the sweat from his forehead with the back of his hand. ''You're mine, baby.'' His eyes glittered again.

Francesca considered denying it. But she was winded.

And aroused.

And he was right.

Cake was being served when they slipped out a side gate. Under cover of loud laughter, nobody seemed to notice them leaving early. Her wrist wrapped by Brett's hard hand, Francesca spared one backward glance and didn't see any member of her family except Carlo, who stood alone, inspecting the melting ice in a cooler.

A whole bucketful couldn't reduce the steaming temperature in Brett's car. Though he flipped on the AC full blast, Francesca knew it wasn't the air that was so hot, but the desire running between them. His hand moved possessively over her upper thigh.

A shiver edged up her spine. ''Brett—''

''No talking,'' he said. ''We'll be there soon.''

Her pulse started slamming against her wrists, her throat. She felt it thrumming low in her body, too, in the spot just above Brett's hand.

His tires whined as he whipped into the apartment parking lot. They were out of the car in seconds, and he was pulling her along in the direction of his apartment.

For a moment, just a moment, it reminded her of the

night before, when he'd been so intent on teaching her a lesson. As they reached his front door, her heart leaped into her throat and she coughed.

He halted, looking down at her. That sparkling glitter hadn't left his eyes, and his gaze was hot as he ran it over her. "Okay?"

She wasn't sure. How bad an idea was it to make love with him again? "I'm—sticky," she said, by way of stalling.

His gaze narrowed, and she didn't think he was going to let her get away so easily. "I have soap and water," he said.

Francesca shuffled back, toward her own apartment. "I can—my place—maybe later—"

He shook his head. "No, Francesca." Then without letting her go he unlocked his door.

Still without releasing her, he drew her toward his bedroom. He passed the bed without even glancing at it and pulled her into his bathroom.

In no time he'd adjusted the shower to a steaming spray. Then he looked at her.

"I, uh…" She gestured toward the door. "I'll let you know when I'm done."

He smiled, knowing and certain as his hands grasped the hem of her top. "I'm sure you will." He whipped the fabric over her head, then reached for the waistband button of her pants.

As he stripped her of her clothes he also stripped her of her will to resist. Clothes gone, he ran his hands over every bare inch of her, and then, after removing his own clothing, he stepped them into the shower and ran the soap over the very same paths.

Once her skin squeaked he washed her hair, and she moaned as he massaged her scalp. Then, as the water ran cooler and cooler, he pushed her up against the tiled wall and chased the twin coursing streams of water down her puckering nipples until they became one river at her navel. He navigated that too, following it lower and lower, until, as he'd promised, Francesca *did* scream.

And she screamed with pleasure again on his big bed a little while later, with Brett deep inside her and with all her doubts and fears drowned in the entwined carnal and emotional sensations of loving Brett.

10

FRANCESCA TRIED not to look gift sex in the mouth. That's how she thought of it, each time she and Brett came together after the day of the barbecue—a gift. One that she might have to pay for in heartache at some later date, but a present she wasn't going to regret now.

She wriggled a bit against Brett's mattress, burrowing her head more comfortably against his shoulder. When he'd come home from work he'd found her in the parking lot, making a minor repair to the gate leading to the apartments. He had something to show her in his apartment, he'd said. She'd left her tools behind and followed him, only to end up making quick and passionate love the instant they'd locked the door.

She still had her shoes on and her T-shirt, her bra unhooked beneath it. Frowning, Francesca ran her palm over Brett's bare chest. "Hey," she said. "What was it you wanted to show me?"

He might have dozed off. But then one eye half opened. "What?"

"You got me out of the parking lot and into your apartment because you said you had something to show me," she reminded him.

Both his eyes opened wide. "Francesca. Honey." His hair brushed against the white pillowcase as he moved his head from side to side in amazement.

She pulled her brows together. "What?"

He was shaking his head again. "You are just too cute."

"What?"

"I said that to you because—" He started to laugh. "I thought you knew what I meant." He laughed harder.

Francesca was beginning to feel like the butt of a joke. "The only thing I know is that I'm sitting here half-naked and you're laughing at me!"

He tried to get serious. She could see him drawing the edges of his mouth together, but then it became too much and he was grinning again. "That's because I brought you here to show you my, uh, my...etchings." He hooted again.

It started to dawn. "Etchings?" she repeated suspiciously.

He sobered up, but the laughter was still brimming in his annoyingly bright blue eyes. "Etchings. You know. Tools? Jewels?"

Heat burned Francesca's cheeks. "I get it now," she said, moving away from Brett's side. "I must seem pretty naive to you." Other women he'd known would have understood his innuendo right away. Gotten the joke.

He rolled close. "You're right about *pretty*." One finger stroked her cheek. "And *naive*."

She barely registered his touch, instead looking down at herself. Her oversize T-shirt nearly reached her knees, but had a half-dollar-sized rip at her navel. Then there was the matter of the shoes. Other women would have gone to a man's bed wearing shiny pumps or delicate sandals that could be toed off. She'd broken a lace this morning and had knotted her right sneaker on. In her hurry to be in Brett's arms she'd merely pulled her shorts and panties right over them.

All the gaucheness and awkwardness she'd ever felt about men and romance returned with a vengeance, cooling her skin like buckets of cold water. She shivered and rolled farther from Brett, just wanting to get back to her own apartment.

His hand clamped on her shoulder. "Where are you going?"

"I…"

He hauled her back against him. "What's going on?"

"I just thought I'd go home now."

Brett stroked her hair away from her face. "Did I say or do something to hurt you?"

Mute, she just shook her head.

He squinted at her. "I did. You didn't like me laughing at you."

"I *am* naive," Francesca found herself whispering.

He rolled her over on top of him and held her against his body. "Not naive. Just innocent. And don't think for a moment that I don't like it," he said.

She frowned, and he rubbed at the spot between her

brows with his thumb. "Francesca," he chided her gently. "I do."

But what did he think about her scuffed and still-on shoes? What did he think about the rip in her shirt? The unladylike way she could *almost* beat him at one-on-one? Insecurity tore through her again.

Not that insecurity was a stranger. Even though she and Brett had been spending every night together, she hadn't told anyone, not her brothers, not Elise, that they were even the most casual of items. She'd tried telling herself it was because she didn't want to jinx what felt so right. She'd tried telling herself it was because she didn't want her brothers to interfere in any way.

Lies.

She'd been silent about it because she didn't know where she stood with him.

Yes, she loved him. Yes, she'd willingly gone into his arms because even this little taste of Brett seemed worthwhile. But now she wasn't so sure.

"Francesca." He jiggled her in his arms, turning his head to find her gaze. "Talk to me."

"Maybe we shouldn't see each other anymore." The words popped out of her mouth.

Brett's eyes narrowed. He sat silent for a moment, staring at her. "Why?" he finally said.

She shrugged, trying not to think about the breathtaking feel of his heart beating against hers. "I don't know. I'm going to be busy in the next few days. The rehearsal for Elise's wedding. The rehearsal dinner. The wedding itself.''

Steeling herself, she focused on his raised left eyebrow. ''You haven't forgotten I'm a bridesmaid.''

In the blink of an eye, he reversed their positions. ''I haven't forgotten,'' he said, his voice almost angry.

With raw power, Brett pressed her into the mattress and insinuated his hips between her legs. ''Exactly what about being a bridesmaid makes you too busy for me?''

Francesca could barely breathe. Not because of Brett's weight, but because she wanted him so very much. Wanted him *forever.*

She swallowed. ''I just have…things to do.'' *Such as protecting my heart. Better late than never.*

''Why can't we do them together?'' he asked. ''I'm invited to the wedding.''

Francesca didn't know how to answer. Was he suggesting they attend the wedding as a couple? In front of Pop and everybody? ''Well, um…''

''And that rehearsal dinner. Isn't it usually customary for the members of the wedding party to bring an escort?''

Francesca wet her lips. ''You mean, kind of like a boyfriend—'' She stopped herself hastily. ''Or a date?''

''Exactly,'' he said. ''Exactly like a date.''

Exactly like a date. In front of Pop and everybody.

She reached up to kiss Brett. If she'd been wearing the rhinestone tiara she couldn't have felt more like a princess.

BRETT SHOWED up at the chapel where Elise and David's wedding would take place three days later. From a side door, he slipped into a pew, taking in that the rehearsal was already underway. David and his four groomsmen, one of whom was Carlo, were lined up beside the white-collared minister. Elise and her attendants were nowhere to be seen.

The minister nodded to the organist, who began playing something soft and soulful. At the back of the chapel a pretty young woman appeared and then walked in measured steps up the aisle. Clutched in her hands appeared to be a paper plate covered with vari-colored gift bows.

He must not be the only dense male in the audience—a pew away a woman whispered to another man that it was a pretend bouquet made from the ribbons on the gifts at Elise's wedding showers. Another young woman started up the aisle with another bow bouquet. Then another woman.

Then, finally, Francesca.

Brett slid forward on the wooden seat. Francesca, making one of her rare appearances in a short dress and high heels, was offering a long drink of her bared legs. His heart rocketed—*slam*—against his chest.

He followed her with his eyes. She'd taken more careful pains with her appearance, her eyelashes sootier than usual and her lips the same rosy color as the soft fabric of her dress.

A primitive, caveman urge rose in him. Brett wanted to take her out of everyone else's sight and take her home. He wanted to peel the dress off her, uncover her golden skin, kiss that rosy mouth and set his blood on fire with the feel and the taste of Francesca.

Bending her head, she looked down at her bouquet and smiled.

Instantly the blood in Brett's veins stopped moving. Something about the sight of Francesca and that bouquet—she held one made up of pure, virginal white ribbons—shut down the pumping ability of his heart. Dizzy, he sucked in a breath.

Why did that damn bouquet terrify him? Why was he suddenly afraid of Francesca?

The rest of the rehearsal passed in a haze. Brett slumped against the hard back of the pew and stared at his knuckles and then his palms and then his knuckles again. He didn't want to watch Francesca. Couldn't.

At the end of the rehearsal the bridesmaids and groomsmen were coupled and filed down the aisle. Still stupid with the weird feeling of dread, it took Brett a few minutes to realize they weren't returning to the main part of the chapel. He finally rose, knowing he had to find Francesca and talk to her.

She was laughing and talking to Carlo. Her brother had that edgy look about him again, but Francesca didn't seem to notice it. "You're going to owe *me* Saturday, big brother," she said. "Don't forget your wallet."

They were talking about that damn bet. A hot bubble rose from Brett's gut. That damn bet was the source of it all. Francesca looking for a man. Francesca in his bed.

Francesca walking up an aisle carrying a white bouquet and looking like everything he'd vowed never to be hurt by again.

Carlo was shaking his head, his mood obviously black. "Give up, Franny. You don't have a prayer."

Her brother's disregard of her feelings, and her appeal, set a torch to Brett's already-simmering anger. He reached them in two strides. "Hell, Carlo. You're the one who should give up. You might as well settle that bet right here and now. I'll lend you the hundred bucks myself."

Two pairs of astonished Italian eyes turned on him. The temperature of Brett's anger instantly dropped. *Uh-oh.*

Francesca opened her mouth, closed it, opened her mouth again. "You know about our bet? How do you know about our bet?"

Brett decided on silence as the best answer.

Carlo narrowed his eyes. "I remember. You showed up at Pop's right after the fact."

With the weight of Francesca's gaze on him, Brett tried shrugging casually. "Yeah. Well."

Another moment of silence, then Francesca looked at her brother. "Go away, Carlo."

His forehead creased. "I don't—"

"Go away, Carlo," she said again.

With one reluctant backward look, Carlo wandered off.

She turned back to Brett, and there was a flush on her cheeks. "You overheard us that day?"

He could hardly deny it at this point. "Yeah."

She rubbed at her temple. She'd painted her nails again, and they were done more expertly now. Brett liked it better when she smeared them a bit.

"You wouldn't—" Her fingers pressed against her temple again. "You didn't do all this because…because of the bet, did you?"

He took a breath. "I couldn't even bring myself to believe you were old enough to date."

She took a step back. "It *was* because of the bet."

"You could get into a lot of trouble out there," he said, frowning at her and defending his logic. "When you're looking for a man to win a bet."

"Rescuing me again, Brett?"

He shrugged.

"Or maybe you felt *sorry* for me."

"No." He shook his head quickly. "I've never felt sorry for you."

Her expression hardened to a coolness he'd never seen before. "What would you call it then? How you feel about me."

In his pockets, his hands balled into fists. "Francesca—"

"I want to know." Still holding that funky bouquet, she crossed her arms over her chest. "Tell me. Or let me try to guess. At first you thought you needed to rescue me. So you asked me out on that date. And then—

and then—'' She halted. ''And then I asked you to make love to me. Practically forced you to.''

''I wanted you, Francesca,'' he said quietly.

''In your bed,'' she added.

A long silence welled between them. Then Francesca drew in a deep breath, held it for a moment, let it out. ''So what would you call what you feel for me now?'' she asked. ''Desire?''

He hated the bitter note in her voice. It made him angry all over again, because from the very beginning, for her entire life, all he'd wanted to do was protect her. From the very kind of hurt he now saw on her face.

''Come on, Brett.'' Her voice taunted him. ''Desire? Or should we just call it plain old lust?''

Goaded, he snapped back. ''Francesca, what did you expect?''

She blinked. ''I thought it might be love,'' she said quietly, then paused. ''Just like what I feel for you.''

He thought the top of his head might come off. *''What?''* he said, dread and anger twining in his belly. ''What the hell are you talking about?''

She bit her lower lip.

Deliberately flexing his fingers, he forced himself to calm down. ''Francesca,'' he said, his voice softer. ''You're confused. What we have together—how good the sex is, that's not love.''

He saw her swallow. ''So it's just a physical thing?'' she said. ''That's what you think?''

''I'm certain.'' He reached out to touch her, but she

backed another step away. "Haven't I always taken care of you? Taught you things you need to know?"

Her face was still a stony mask.

"So let me teach you something else. Don't be so quick to claim love. Love hurts, Francesca. Don't go looking for it."

He clenched his teeth, wishing he didn't need to say it. Wishing she hadn't wanted to change what they had.

"We're through," she said abruptly.

Brett ran a hand through his hair. "Francesca."

"I don't want your pity or your protection anymore."

He shook his head. "It doesn't have to be this way. It doesn't have to end. We're good together."

"But we're not in love with each other."

He shook his head again.

"Goodbye, Brett." As dignified as royalty, she inclined her head in a nod and walked away from him, her back straight and her shoulders square.

She approached the group of people that included Carlo. Putting her hand through his arm, she drew her brother away. Guilt surged through Brett as he noticed her tight hold on Carlo.

Damn if he didn't feel as if he'd just burst the brightest balloon in the sky.

IN A BOOTH at a cheesy chain coffee shop, Francesca sat across from her brother, nursing a cup of decaf from a thick white mug. "I'm having a romantic crisis," she said. "And you bring me to a place like this?" Better to complain than to cry.

Carlo raised his brows. "A latte would make you feel better?"

Francesca sighed. "Guess not." She propped her elbow on the plastic tabletop and rested her chin against her fist. "Do you think I did the right thing?" She'd told her brother the entire story, well, not the *entire* story, but enough for him to get the picture.

He shrugged. Beside a few grunts, he'd been pretty silent about the whole thing.

"That's *all* you have to say? I'm giving you a chance for an 'I told you so,' you know."

Carlo smiled ruefully. "If I thought it would make either one of us feel better, I'd say it."

She frowned at him. "I'm not a quitter, Carlo, you know that. Yes, I gave Brett the big heave-ho, but if you think there's a chance, something I could say that would—"

Carlo was already shaking his head. "Forget it, Francesca."

"Forget it?" she echoed. This wasn't why she'd un loaded her troubles on him. In the time that it took to drive to the coffee place, she decided she'd probably acted too hastily. "You're supposed to help me!" Carlo had to help her concoct a plan.

He drained the black and lethal-looking stuff in his mug, then shrugged.

She eyed him with sudden interest, for the first time

noticing he'd lost weight and there were shadows under his eyes. "You've been acting strangely for the past few months. What's going on with *you?*"

"Nothing."

She sat up straight. "Don't give me that. Are you having a problem at work?"

He shook his head. "No, Franny. But I appreciate the concern."

Carlo was really starting to worry her. She'd taken a chance revealing her relationship with Brett to Carlo, especially after that punch he'd given him a few weeks ago. But she needed to talk to someone, and this was not the time to share romantic troubles with her best friend, an imminent bride.

She looked at her brother's stony expression and sighed. "Maybe I *should* have talked to Elise."

Something flickered in Carlo's eyes.

A weird thought entered Francesca's mind, and her heart stuttered. No. *No.*

But Carlo's mood had darkened at the same time that Elise's wedding preparations had really begun. But no. He'd known David and Elise their entire lives. He wouldn't…

"Carlo." She reached across the table and touched her brother's hand. "You—you're one of the grooms-men. David is one of your best friends."

"Correct," he said, in that maddeningly cool, police detective way of his.

"They're very happy," Francesca went on. "Perfect for each other."

"Correct," he said again, his face giving away nothing.

Francesca felt a little desperate. She wanted to believe such a thing couldn't happen. Walking the relationship tightrope with Brett made her want to be certain of a big, cushy, happy-ending net below. But something told her the truth.

"You love her," Francesca said, the words hard to force out. "You love Elise."

Nothing changed on Carlo's face. "With every breath I take."

"Oh, *Carlo*."

His eyes bore into hers. "But that's just between us. Our secret. You get it, Franny? I don't want to burden David *or* Elise with this, ever."

She nodded dumbly. Carlo loved Elise. Elise loved David. No, no, no. Breath shuddered into her lungs. "Why? Why are you telling me this now?"

Carlo raised his brows. "See if you can figure it out."

She had stomped away from Brett half mad, half maudlin. She'd captured Carlo, hoping he would talk some sense into her or at least help her make sense of Brett's distrust of love. Carlo was going to help her forge a plan, she'd thought, because…because…because the simple truth was that she was in love and wanted to be loved back.

Carlo loved Elise. Elise loved David. Francesca loved Brett. Brett didn't want to be in love.

"I thought it was going to be flowers and champagne. Satin sheets and shiny rings."

"I know," Carlo said.

But that's what she wanted it to be! That's the dream she'd always had. The one she'd tossed off her sneakers and her blue jeans to find. It had to be out there!

But Carlo loved Elise. Elise loved David. Francesca loved Brett. Brett didn't want to be in love.

Francesca sighed. "But love's a lot more complicated than roses and rides in limousines, isn't it? Lots more potential for heartbreak."

Carlo gave her another rueful smile. "Isn't that what Brett's already figured out?"

And she'd thought men stuck to bachelorhood because they didn't want to pick up their socks. What a silly fool she'd been. Accepting defeat, Francesca slumped against the back of her red vinyl seat.

11

WEDGED IN A CORNER of a crowded pew, Brett caught himself craning his neck for a glimpse of the bridesmaids. *Damn.* He whipped back around, massaging a cramp in his shoulder.

What was he trying to do? Who was he trying to see? Couldn't be Francesca. She'd made her choice, and he was fine with it. So what if he hadn't slept the past two nights. The problem had nothing to do with the big hole she'd left on one side of his bed.

A hand clamped on his shoulder. He jerked his gaze upward to meet the serious brown eyes of Carlo. Dressed in a dark tuxedo, he was escorting a behatted woman to a seat in the pew behind him.

The woman slid into place, and Carlo squeezed his shoulder. "How you doing?" he asked.

Brett shot him a wary glance, then looked pointedly at the hand still heavy on him. "Fine. Relaxed. Well rested." All lies.

Carlo left his hand where it was and raised his brows. "That so?"

"Yeah." The Milano family had nothing to do with his mood.

''I thought maybe you were…hurting.''

Yeah, right. And if he just happened to tell Carlo that his sister was the cause of that hurt and exactly *where* it ached, then Brett could be sure to be reintroduced to at least five of her brother's knuckles. ''I'm fine, Carlo.''

His only real complaint was sleep deprivation.

Carlo gave one more squeeze to his shoulder, hard enough to make Brett wince. Then he returned to the back of the church.

Brett massaged his arm to loosen his shoulder while the wedding procession began. David and his grooms-men were up front, and just like at the rehearsal, the organist began to play processional music. The first of the bridesmaids passed Brett, wearing a simple white gown.

Did bridesmaids usually wear white? Brett shrugged. Apparently Elise liked the color because the two brides-maids following wore it as well.

He looked back, just to verify the color of the dress of bridesmaid number four.

Francesca.

The vision of her hit his eyes like a blinding flash. His breath sucked in sharply. Out of his life for two days, and somehow he'd forgotten how beautiful she was. Sleeveless and white, the dress revealed the golden perfection of her shoulders then went on to hug the gen-erous curves of her breasts and the slender lines of her waist and hips.

Closing his eyes, he turned back around in his seat.

Some sensation weighed on his chest, but he ignored it, promising himself a tall beer and a good rest when he got home.

He didn't need to open his eyes to know when she passed his pew. Her perfume, that one she'd had him vet weeks ago, reached him first. The heaviness on his chest increased.

Two beers and a good rest.

The rest of the ceremony went by in a haze. Elise and David must have said the right things, because fairly soon it was over. Brett stood in his pew, shuffling forward as he followed the crowd out of the chapel.

Maybe he'd skip the reception. But what was the likelihood of finding sleep? Gauging the answer as *None,* he dutifully followed the directions to the reception. He didn't hesitate at the receiving line, either, shaking David's hand in congratulations and kissing Elise on the cheek.

Halfway down the line stood bridesmaid number four, and up close he could see someone had performed an elaborate and sophisticated makeup job on her. "Francesca," he said, his voice tight.

"Brett. How've you been?"

No telling what she was thinking behind the dramatic sweep of her eyelashes and the reddened curve of her lips. His hand curled into an involuntary fist. "Great," he said. "I've been great."

She smiled, looking past him to the person following closely behind. He'd been dismissed.

What the hell.

He found the bar and ordered a whisky. Neat.

The reception proceeded as all do. Food. Dancing. Brett drank.

Using the dance band's microphone, the best man made a toast.

Francesca, as maid of honor, grabbed it next. She brought it toward her mouth, and the thing squealed reverb so loudly Brett thought maybe she'd burst his eardrums.

Everyone else laughed, shook their heads and then quieted for Francesca's short speech.

Brett couldn't hear it. His ears were still ringing. That weight on his chest grew heavier by the minute. He thought he was coming down with something.

No wonder he hadn't been sleeping.

Next came the obligatory garter throw. Brett stayed out of the running, instead nursing another whisky.

Elise prepared to throw her bouquet. Jostling and laughing with embarrassment, a whole passel of single women lined up for the chance to be the next designated bride. Veil floating behind her, Elise turned her back, then checked over her shoulder.

Whatever she saw caused her to abandon her position and stamp away. In seconds she was back, Francesca in tow. Rolling her eyes, Francesca broke free and stood at the very back of the grouped women, obviously uninterested in catching the bouquet.

Brett found himself moving forward. Just to get a bet-

Lotto

Win a dream holiday on the
Holiday Bonanza scratchcard
014-11188652-01429

```
A.  02 11 15 22 25 40
B.  02 11 15 19 22 28
C.  01 07 25 30 32 44
D.  07 15 25 27 38 47
E.  02 06 19 22 25 37
```

SAT17 JAN 04
FOR 01 SAT DRAW

028645 RET NO. 112757 £ 5.00
014-11188652-01429
FILL BOX TO VOID

GO

THE NATIONAL LOTTERY®

For information about The National Lottery please call the National Lottery Line on 0845 910 0000, or visit our website at www.national-lottery.co.uk. A separate MINICOM line for the hard of hearing is also available.
More than 28% of National Lottery proceeds is expected to go to the Good Causes over the period of Camelot's operating licence.

GUIDANCE ON HOW TO PLAY

The name(s) of the game(s) for which this ticket is issued is/are printed overleaf. For how to play and prize structures see the Players' Guide, available from Retailers or the National Lottery Line.
The results can be found through recognised media channels, National Lottery On-Line Retailers or the National Lottery Line.
Tickets issued in error, illegible or incomplete can be cancelled if returned to the issuing terminal within 120 minutes after purchase and before close of ticket sales from that terminal on that day.

GUIDANCE ON HOW TO CLAIM A PRIZE

For details about how and where to claim prizes of various values see the Players' Guide, available at Retailers. If you hold a winning ticket you must claim your prize by post, or in person at a National Lottery Retailer, Post Office or Regional Centre as appropriate, within 180 days of the applicable draw date, or within this period notify the National Lottery Line of your intention to claim, and then claim within 187 days of that draw date.
Claims of over £50,000 must be made in person. **If you believe you have won over £50,000 telephone the National Lottery Line.** For all claims over £500 you will be required to complete a claim form available from a Retailer or by telephoning the National Lottery Line, and show proof of identity. To claim by post, please send your ticket and completed claim form(where required), at your own risk, to The National Lottery, P.O. Box 287, Watford WD18 9TT.

GO

Name _____

Address _____

_____ Post Code _____

Safe custody of your ticket is your responsibility. If your ticket is lost, stolen, or destroyed, you can make a written claim to Camelot no later than 30 days after the winning draw date, but it will be at Camelot's discretion whether or not to investigate and to pay the claim.

THE OPERATOR OF THE NATIONAL LOTTERY

The National Lottery is run by Camelot Group plc under licence granted by the National Lottery Commission. The principal office of the National Lottery Operator, Camelot Group plc is The National Lottery, Tolpits Lane, Watford WD18 9RN.

GAMES RULES AND PROCEDURES

The game(s) for which this ticket is issued is/are subject to the Rules and Procedures for that game/those games, which set out the contractual rights and obligations of the player and the game(s) promoter (and operator if different). Game(s) Rules and Procedures are available to view at National Lottery On-Line games Retailers, and copies can be obtained from the National Lottery Line. The promoter/operator is entitled to treat this ticket as invalid if the data hereon does not correspond with the entries on Camelot's central computer. Players must be 16 or over.

GO

THE NATIONAL LOTTERY®

For information about The National Lottery please call the National Lottery Line on 0845 910 0000, or visit o website at www.national-lottery.co.uk. A separate MINICOM line for the hard of hearing is also available.
More than 28% of National Lottery proceeds is expected to go to the Good Causes over the period of Camelot's operating licence.

ter view of the action. Then, with a big show of a wind-up, Elise let the bouquet fly.

Obviously the sports gene wasn't going to be passed to Elise and David's future children on the maternal side. The flowers went high and long, flying nearer to Brett than any of the single ladies, who, in their best dresses and heels, didn't have a prayer of grabbing the thing.

But he'd forgotten the one woman raised by four older brothers. Four brothers who'd honed in her a competitive streak impossible to suppress. Four brothers who'd shown a girl how to move, and she sure could do it, since she'd exchanged her high heels for a pair of high-top sneakers.

Francesca faded back, nearly bumping into him. Brett tried to give her more room, but with a table and chairs behind him, his movements were restricted.

The bouquet was still sailing high on a collision course for the wall. Certainly no one could reach it. Then Francesca jumped, her body bowing in the best running back style. The flowers landed in her arms.

Francesca landed against Brett's chest. He went backward.

To save herself from falling with him, she dug her elbows into his ribs.

''Oomph!'' With a scatter of crowd and chairs, Brett landed, hard and alone, on the polished parquet floor.

Safely on her two feet, Francesca peered down at him, the flowers cradled in her arms. ''Oops,'' she said.

She didn't look the least bit sorry. But he didn't *think*

she intentionally meant to step on his hand as she turned her back on him and walked away.

Chest heaving, Brett lay sprawled on the floor. His neck cramp was back. His shoulders ached from the Carlo squeeze. His ribs hurt. His back hurt. His fingers, the ones Francesca had crushed beneath her sneaker, throbbed.

But not one of the pains was anything, compared to the pain of seeing her once again walk away. The realization struck him with the force of an atomic explosion.

Carlo reached his side. He clasped Brett's hand and pulled him to his feet. ''You okay, pal?''

''I hurt like hell,'' Brett told his friend seriously.

Carlo frowned. ''You need a doctor?''

Brett rubbed a palm over his chest. ''I don't think that will help.''

He'd called it sleep deprivation. He'd puzzled over the ache in his chest and the strange pain that the sight of Francesca had inflicted on his eyes.

Well, he'd figured it out now.

Somewhere, somehow, some way, the lady in the sneakers, who'd been his tomboy princess, had grown up to become the queen of his heart.

God, it sounded so corny but it felt so true.

He loved her. He was in love with her.

And all the hurt he'd been so afraid to risk by loving her was nothing compared to the pain of living without her.

He looked over at his best friend. "Damn, Carlo. I've been a fool."

Francesca's brother smiled. "My thoughts exactly."

SHE'D DISAPPEARED. Brett forced himself to slowly retrace his steps.

No Francesca on the dance floor.

She wasn't hanging by the wedding cake.

The head table, reserved for the wedding party, was empty.

He walked the perimeter of the large room again, stopping by the bar for another whisky to quell his panic.

He needed to talk to her. Now. His heart was alive and well, and he had to tell her about it.

Stumped, he went outside.

It only took him a few minutes to spot a pair of size-five sneakers loitering around the back bumper of a newly washed car decorated with Just Married signs and tissue paper flowers. A bulging garbage bag at her feet, Francesca stood, frowning at a ball of twine in her hands.

"Need help?" he asked.

She jumped then looked up. "*You.*"

"You" didn't think she was feeling very charitable toward him.

He took a breath. "What are you doing?"

"Tying some tin cans together. Then tying them to Elise and David's bumper."

Brett took another deep breath. "Patricia and I never set a wedding date," he said.

Francesca sent him a startled look, then bent her head over the twine.

''I was thinking about that today. Thinking about why we didn't set the date.'' Brett took a swallow from his glass of whisky. ''And it wasn't because it takes five years to plan a wedding.''

''I don't think I want to hear any more,'' Francesca said.

''But I need to talk about it. I need to tell you—to explain.''

Her fingers stopped fiddling with the string.

''When she died,'' he went on, ''it was terrible. I couldn't get over what a waste it was. This beautiful, vibrant young woman. I couldn't get over what she *hadn't* experienced. She'd never been a wife. Never held her child in her arms.''

Francesca hugged herself. ''I *really* don't want to hear any more.''

Brett moved closer to her, gripping his whisky tightly in his hand. ''And I felt guilty because I didn't regret she hadn't been *my* wife. That she hadn't had *my* child.''

There were tears in Francesca's dark eyes. ''What are you saying?''

''I'm not sure exactly. I'm just trying to tell you how it was. Patricia and I…we'd been part of each other's lives since we were seventeen. We went to college together. Then law school. When it seemed like it was time to get engaged, we did that together, too.''

''But you loved her,'' Francesca whispered.

Brett nodded. "I did. And I'd give anything to have her back in the world." He inhaled a long breath and then admitted something he'd kept secret for almost two years. "But I don't think I would have married her. And in many ways, knowing that has made her death more painful."

Francesca swiped at her eyes with the back of one hand. Then she kneeled by the bag and started taking out tin cans. "Why are you telling me all this, Brett?"

Whump. Whump. Whump. His heart started a bass drum beat in his chest. Talking about the past was easy. "Because...because I want you to know why taking a chance on the future is pretty hard for me, Francesca."

She lined up the empty cans in perfect rows. Tuna size on the left. Chicken noodle on the right. "I've been disappointed too, Brett."

She didn't have to say that he'd been the one to hurt her. He hunkered down beside her, trying to get her to look at him. "I know it's my fault. And I'm sorry Francesca." *Whump. Whump. Whump.* "But I've figured it out now."

She looked up, her gaze suspicious. "Figured out what?"

"I'd regret it like hell if I let you go. I won't let you become someone else's wife. The only child I want to see you carrying is mine. *Ours.*"

Whump. Whump. Whump. His heart beat so loudly he thought he might have to read her lips. Her head stayed bent over the cans.

"I love you," he said, desperate for her to respond.

She rearranged the cans, and he could see her hands shaking. "You said you wouldn't have married Patricia. But you two were engaged when she died. Why?"

He shrugged. "I suppose because I didn't want to hurt her feelings by breaking it off. And I think she didn't want to hurt mine, either."

One last can plunked to the asphalt. Francesca kept her hand curled over its open edge as she looked at Brett. "But, see, there's the rub."

His heart almost stopped.

"Since I was a little girl, you've been the one to make things better for me," Francesca said. "My protector. My knight."

Brett couldn't deny it.

"And you know I felt bad the other day when you said you didn't love me."

She looked down at the can, and he could see her fingers tighten on it. "How do I know you're not saying this for the same reason you stayed with Patricia?"

Before he could respond, she let out a startled cry. Her hand on the can opened, and he could see a long slice crossing three fingers and welling blood.

"God, Francesca." He grabbed the palm of her hand and pulled her to her feet. "Let's go find a first aid kit and some disinfectant."

She stubbornly resisted him and slipped her hand out of his, her eyes angry. "No. I hate that stinging stuff as much as I hate your pity, Brett."

''Francesca, let's get this cleaned. We can argue later.''

She shook her head, her shoes digging post holes into the asphalt, her hand dripping blood. ''No. I don't like disinfectant.''

Exasperated, Brett moved to run his hand through his hair, only to discover he was still holding the glass of whisky. He looked at the two inches of alcohol in the glass. He eyed the stubborn, sexy, tomboy love of his life. From the top of her sleek dark head to the bottom of her scuffed sneakers she was every chance he needed to take…every bit of life he had to reach out for.

''Let's recap,'' he said, advancing on her. ''You're afraid I said I love you because I don't want to hurt you.''

She didn't see it coming. She didn't even try to resist when Brett grabbed Francesca's bleeding hand and in one deft move poured the contents of his glass—whisky, one hundred proof—over the cut.

She gasped in pain. He smiled.

''But now you see, honey,'' he said. ''That point is moot.''

''Brett.'' Tears turned Francesca's eyes to dark crystals, and he knew she believed him. He pulled her into his arms to kiss the tears, to kiss her mouth, to whisper in her ear that he loved her for all time and was never going to let her go.

''Just try,'' she said, the tears gone and that tomboy gleam back in her eye.

He grinned and held her close to his heart. "I'm afraid."

"Good," she said. "I want you to be afraid. Be *very* afraid."

And Brett was. It scared him that he'd almost turned his back on such happiness.

FRANCESCA automatically moved her feet in the old-fashioned dance steps. Over her father's shoulder, she held out her left hand and admired the wedding band now snuggled close to the engagement ring Brett had slipped on her hand four months ago. She'd only wanted the band, but once they'd shared their news with Pop he'd insisted on giving them her mother's diamond solitaire.

Knowing how happy her parents had been together, it only seemed fitting.

Her veil drifted over Pop's sleeve, and she reached up to adjust her headpiece. Brett had smiled so tenderly when he'd seen it. She'd had it especially made, delicate white tulle attached to the tiara he'd given her that magical night.

Speaking of nights...she sighed. It would be hours before she could be alone with Brett. The reception was going to last *forever*. Her brothers and Pop had turned startlingly romantic on her and sworn they wouldn't feel right if she didn't have a fancy wedding with every trimming known to man, er, wedding planner.

Her Aunt Elizabetta, dear sweet Sister Josephine

Mary, had crocheted tiny bags for each guest, which held the traditional Italian good-luck almonds. If those didn't get her great-aunt into heaven, Francesca didn't know what would.

Rising on tiptoe, Francesca looked over her father's shoulders to survey the other dancers. All the brothers had been pressed into Fred Astaire service. Only old Fred never looked as pained as the four tuxedoed men shuffling across the dance floor. She shook her head. They needed women to whip them into shape, but she was sidestepping the job to concentrate on the man who'd taken her heart as easily as he'd taken her up on his bicycle all those years ago.

She loved her husband so very much.

Movement at the edge of the dance floor caught her eye. Brett. She grinned, squiggling her fingers at him in a little wave. He waved back, then pointed to the bowl of sugared almonds on the table beside him. As she watched, he scooped up a huge handful of them and stored them in his already-bulging side pocket.

A little shiver ran down Francesca's spine. Somehow he'd gotten the Italian almond tradition all wrong. Though she'd tried to correct him and explain it was a fertility charm, he insisted it was a sexual charm and claimed he was going to give her a climax for every almond he left the wedding with.

She blew Brett a kiss. It was hard to argue with such a delightful idea.

MILLS & BOON®

Makes
any time
special

Enjoy a romantic novel from
Mills & Boon®

Presents...™   Enchanted™   TEMPTATION.

Historical Romance™   ⚕MEDICAL
ROMANCE

THE

Regency

COLLECTION

Where rogues find romance

**Look out for the tenth volume in this limited
collection of Regency Romances from
Mills & Boon® in February 2000.**

Featuring:

Eleanor
by Sylvia Andrew

and

Miss Weston's Masquerade
by Francesca Shaw

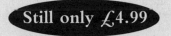

Still only £4.99

MILLS & BOON®

Makes any time special™

COMING NEXT MONTH

THE NINE-MONTH BRIDE by Judy Christenberry

Susannah longed for a baby and Lucas desperately wanted a son, but not the emotional ties of marriage. So they decided to make a convenient marriage, then make a baby - the old-fashioned way…

THE BOSS AND THE BEAUTY by Donna Clayton

Cindy was determined to make her boss, Kyle, see her as a woman rather than his employee. But as Kyle *never* mixed business with pleasure—it was going to be a long haul to get this man from the boardroom to the altar!

TAMING JASON by Lucy Gordon

Jason was injured and temporarily blind, and for his sake Elinor must keep her identity a secret. What would happen when he was able to see her again - and recognise her as the woman he'd once considered unsuitable for marriage?

A HUSBAND WORTH WAITING FOR
by Grace Green

After his accident Jed's memory loss turned him into an entirely different man. Sarah found him charming—even seductive! But how long until Jed's memory returned? And when it did, would he still be a husband worth waiting for?

Available from 4th February 2000

Available at most branches of WH Smith, Tesco, Martins, Borders, Easons, Volume One/James Thin and most good paperback bookshops

COMING NEXT MONTH

MILLS & BOON®

Enchanted™

BORROWED BACHELOR by Barbara Hannay

Maddy needed a man who'd pretend to be her boyfriend, and her sexy neighbour Rick seemed ideal. Yet Rick played the part of the attentive lover so convincingly that even Maddy's mind turned towards marriage…

MEANT FOR YOU by Patricia Knoll

Jed thinks Caitlin is too uptight. She thinks Jed is too laid-back. All they have to do is stick to their separate sides of the house. So why do they keep meeting in the hallway?

MARRYING MARGOT by Barbara McMahon

The worst time in Rand's life had been when he and Margot had lost their baby and their young marriage had floundered. Now Rand wanted a reconciliation and more children. Margot still loved him, but she couldn't go through the heartache again…

THE BILLIONAIRE DADDY by Renee Roszel

Baby Tina needed a mum and her aunt Lauren wanted to take on the role—as soon as she had dealt with Tina's so-called 'father', Dade Delacourt. When Dade mistook Lauren for Tina's nanny the mistake gave Lauren the ideal opportunity to check out Dade's parenting skills. Except the plan backfired because the irresistible billionaire expected her to be with him twenty-four hours a day…

Available from 4th February 2000